George John Whyte-Melville

The White Rose

Vol. 1

George John Whyte-Melville

The White Rose
Vol. 1

ISBN/EAN: 9783337416119

Printed in Europe, USA, Canada, Australia, Japan

Cover: Foto ©Andreas Hilbeck / pixelio.de

More available books at **www.hansebooks.com**

THE WHITE ROSE

BY

G. J. WHYTE MELVILLE,

AUTHOR OF

"CERISE," "THE GLADIATORS," "THE BROOKES OF BRIDLEMERE," ETC.

IN THREE VOLUMES.

VOL. I.

LONDON:

CHAPMAN AND HALL, 193, PICCADILLY.

1868.

CONTENTS.

CHAPTER VII.

CHAPTER VIII.

CHAPTER IX.

CHAPTER X.

CHAPTER XI.

CHAPTER XII.

CHAPTER XIII.

CHAPTER XIV.

THE WHITE ROSE.

CHAPTER I.

THE MAN IN THE STREET.

It was dawn—dawn here in London, almost as cool and clear as in the pleasant country, where the bird was waking in the garden and the tall poplar stirred and quivered in the morning breeze. It was dawn on the bold outline of the inland hills, dawn on the dreary level of the deep, dark sea. Night after night daylight returns to nature, as sorrow after sorrow hope comes back to man. Even in the hospital—say St. George's Hospital, for that was nearest to where I stood—the bright-eyed morning stole in to greet a score of sufferers, who had longed for her coming through weary hours of pain, to welcome her arrival as nurse, physician,

friend; and although on one dead, up-turned face
the grey light shed a greyer, ghastlier gleam—
what then?—a spirit had but broken loose from
last night's darkness, and departed in the tremble
of twilight for the land beyond the grave, the place
of everlasting day.   It was dawn, too, in the long
perspective of the silent streets—silent none the
less for the booted tramp of an occasional policeman,
for the rumble of a belated cab, for shifting figures
flitting like ghosts round distant corners—squalid,
restless, degraded, and covered far too scantily
with aught but shame.   And it was dawn in the
principal rooms of one of the best houses in
London, filled with the great ones of the earth, or
as they term themselves, somewhat presumptuously,
with "none but the best people"—a dawn less
welcome here than in deep copse or breezy up-
land, than on the wide, lone sea, in the hushed
ward of the hospital, or among the narrow streets—
greeted, indeed, as a deliverer only by a few out-
wearied chaperones, and perhaps by the light-
fingered musicians who had still an endless *cotillon*
to work through before they could cover up their
instruments and go to bed.

I had been down to supper—that is to say, I had

stretched my arm over a white shoulder for half-a-tumbler of champagne and seltzer-water (the *latter* good of its kind), and had absorbed most of it in my glove, whilst I ministered at the same time to the wants of a stately dame whom I remember—ah! so long ago—the slimmest and the lightest mover that ever turned a partner's head in a waltz (we did not call them *round dances* then), and whom I now contemplate, when we meet, with mingled feelings of respect, astonishment, and gratitude for deliverance from possible calamity. *She* was not satisfied with champagne and seltzer-water, far from it—though she drank that mixture with gratification too; but wisely restored vitality after the fatigues of the evening by a substantial supper, and I am not sure but that she had earned her provender fairly enough.

"You must take me back now, please," she said, "or the girls won't know where to find me!"

I wonder whether she thought of the time when *her* mamma didn't know where to find *us*, and the scolding she got in the carriage going home. I was sure she must have had it by the black looks and stiff bow I myself encountered in the Park next day.

Dear! dear! was there ever any state of society in which youthful affections, fancies, attachments, call them what you will, were of a material to withstand the wear of a little time, a little absence, a good deal of amusement bordering on dissipation? Would such an Arcadia be pleasant or wearisome, or is it simply impossible? Alas! I know not; but as far as my own observation goes, you may talk of your first love as poetically as you please—it's your *last* love that comes in and makes a clean sweep of every-thing on the board.

I need scarcely observe, this is not the remark I made as we laboured heavily up Lady Billesdon's staircase, and parted at a doorway crowded to suffocation half-an-hour ago, but affording fair ingress and egress now, for the company were departing; hoarse voices announced that carriages "stopped the way," or their owners were "coming out;" while the linkman, with a benevolence beyond all praise, hoped "her Grace had not forgotten him," and that "the young ladies enjoyed their ball!"

It was time for the young ladies to go, unless perhaps they were very young indeed, quite in their first season. Through the open squares of the ball-

room windows a grey gap in the sky, already
tinged with blue, was every moment widening into
day.   Lamps, and bright eyes too, began to wear a
faded lustre, while the pale morning light, creeping
along the passages and staircase, seemed to invade
the company, dancers and all, like some merciless
epidemic from which there was no escape.   Perhaps
this might account for much of the hooding,
wrapping-up, and general hurry of departure.

To a majority of the performers, besides those who
have been fulfilling a duty and are glad it is over, I
am not sure but that this same going away con-
stitutes the pleasantest part of a ball.   In a gathering of which amusement is the ostensible object, it
is strange how many ·of the stronger and more
painful feelings of our nature can be aroused by
causes apparently trivial in themselves, but often
leading to unlooked-for results.   How many a
formal greeting masks a heart that thrills, and a
pulse that leaps, to the tone of somebody's voice, or
the rustle of somebody's dress.   How many a careless inquiry, being interpreted, signifies a volume of
protestation or a torrent of reproach.   With what
electric speed can eager eyes, from distant corners,
flash the expected telegram along the wires of

mutual intelligence, through a hundred unconscious
bystanders, and make two people happy who have
not exchanged one syllable in speech. There is no
end to " the hopes and fears that shake a single
ball;" but it is when the ball is nearly over, and
the cloaking for departure begins, that the hopes
assume a tangible form and the fears are satisfac-
torily dispelled. It is so easy to explain in low,
pleading whispers why such a dance was refused, or
such a cavalier preferred under the frown of authority, or in fear of the *convenances ;* so pleasant to lean
on a strong arm, in a nook not only sheltered from
doorway draughts but a little apart from the stream
of company, while a kind hand adjusts the folds of
the burnous with tender care, to be rewarded by a
hasty touch, a gentle pressure, perhaps a flower,
none the less prized that it has outlived its bloom.
How precious are such moments, and how fleeting !
Happy indeed if protracted ever so little by the
fortunate coincidence of a footman from the country,
a coachman fast asleep on his box, and a carriage
that never comes till long after it has been called !

I stood at the top of Lady Billesdon's staircase
and watched the usual " business " with an attention
partly flagging from weariness, partly diverted in

the contemplation of my hostess herself, whose pluck
and endurance, while they would have done honour to
the youngest Guardsman present, were no less extra-
ordinary than admirable in an infirm old lady of three-
score. Without counting a dinner-party (to meet
Royalty) she had been "under arms," so to speak,
for more than five hours, erect at the doorway of
her own ball-room, greeting her guests, one by one,
as they arrived, with unflagging cordiality, never
missing the bow, the hand-shake, nor the "right
thing" said to each. On her had devolved the
ordering, the arrangements, the whole responsibility
of the entertainment, the invitations accorded—
above all, the invitations denied! And now she
stood before me, that great and good woman, without a quiver of fatigue in her eyelids, an additional
line of care on her quiet matronly brow.

It was wonderful! It must have been something
more than enthusiasm that kept her up, something
of that stern sense of duty which fixed the Roman
soldier at his post when the boiling deluge swept a
whole population before it, and engulphed pleasant,
wicked Pompeii in a sea of fire. But it was her
own kind heart that prompted the hope I had been
amused, and the pleasant "Good-night" with which

she replied to my farewell bow and sincere congratulations (for she was an old friend) on the success of her ball.

Lady Billesdon, and those like her who give large entertainments, at endless trouble and expense, for the amusement of their friends, deserve more gratitude from the charming young people of both sexes who constitute the rising generation of society in London than these are inclined to admit. It is not to be supposed that an elderly lady of orderly habits, even with daughters to marry, can derive much enjoyment from a function which turns her nice house out at windows, and keeps her weary self a-foot and waking till six o'clock in the morning; but if people whose day for dancing has gone by did not thus sacrifice their comfort and convenience to the pleasures of their juniors, I will only ask the latter to picture to themselves what a dreary waste would be the London season, what a desolate round of recurring penance would seem parks, shoppings, operas, and those eternal dinners, unrelieved by a single ball !

Some such reflections as these so engrossed my attention as I went down stairs, mechanically fingering the latch-key in my waistcoat pocket, that I am

ashamed to say I inadvertently trod on the dress of
a lady in front of me, and was only made aware
of my awkwardness when she turned her head, and
with a half-shy, half-formal bow accosted me by
name.

"It is a long time since we have met," she said,
detaching herself for a moment from the arm of a
good-looking man who was taking her to her carriage, while she put her hand out, and added, "but
I hope you have not quite forgotten me."

Forgotten her? a likely thing, indeed, that any
man between sixteen and sixty, who had ever
known Leonora Welby, should forget her while he
retained his senses! I had not presence of mind to
exclaim, as a good-for-nothing friend of mine
always does on such occasions, "I wish I could!"
but, reflecting that I had been three hours in the
same house without recognising her, I bowed over
the bracelet on her white arm, stupefied, and when
I recovered my senses, she had reached the cloak-
room, and disappeared.

"'Gad, how well she looks to-night!" said a
hoarse voice behind me; "none of the young ones
can touch her even now. It's not the same form
you see—not the same form."

"She? who?" I exclaimed; for my wits were still wool-gathering.

"Who? why Mrs. Vandeleur!" was the reply. "You needn't swagger as if you didn't know her, when she turned round on purpose to shake hands with you,—a thing I haven't seen her do for half-a-dozen men this season. I am a good bit over fifty, my boy; and till I've bred a horse that can win the Derby, I don't mean to turn my attention to anything else; but I can tell you, if she did as much for me twice in a week, I shouldn't know whether I was standing on my grey head or my gouty heels. She's a witch—that's what *she* is: and you and I are old enough to keep out of harm's way. Good-night!"

Old Cotherstone was right. She *was* a witch; but how different from, and oh! how infinitely more dangerous than, the witches our forefathers used to gag, and drown, and burn, without remorse. She was coming out of the cloak-room again, still haunted by that good-looking young gentleman, who was probably over head and ears in love with her, and I could stare at her without rudeness now, from my post of observation on the landing. Yes, it was no wonder I had not recognised her; though the dark pencilled eyebrows and the deep-fringed eyes were Norah Welby's, it was hardly possible to believe that this high-bred, queenly, beautiful woman, could be the laughing, light-hearted girl I remembered in her father's parsonage some ten or fifteen years ago.

She was no witch then. She was a splendid enchantress now. There was magic in the gleam that tinged her dark chestnut hair with gold; magic in the turn of her small head, her delicate temples, her chiselled features, her scornful, self-reliant mouth, and the depth of her large, dark, loving eyes. Every movement of the graceful neck, of the tall, lithe figure, of the shapely limbs, denoted pride, indeed, but it was a pride to withstand injury, oppression, misfortune, insult, all the foes that could attack it from without, and to yield only at the softening touch of love.

As she walked listlessly to her carriage, taking, it seemed to me, but little heed of her companion, I imagined I could detect, in a certain weariness of step and gesture, the tokens of a life unsatisfied, a destiny incomplete. I wonder what made me think of Sir Walter Raleigh flinging down his gold embroidered cloak, the only precious thing he possessed, at the feet of the maiden queen? The

young adventurer doubtless acted on a wise calcula-
tion and a thorough knowledge of human, or at
least of feminine, nature ; but there is here and
there a woman in the world for whom a man flings
his very heart down, recklessly and unhesitatingly,
to crush and trample if she will.   Sometimes she
treads it into the mire, but oftener, I think, she
picks it up, and takes it to her own breast, a
cherished prize, purer, better, and holier for the
ordeal through which it has passed.

I had no carriage to take me home, and wanted
none.   No gentle voice when I arrived there, kind
or querulous, as the case might be, to reproach me
with the lateness of the hour.   Shall I say of this
luxury also, that I wanted none ?   No ; buttoning
my coat, and reliant on my latch-key, I passed into
the grey morning and the bleak street, as Mrs.
Vandeleur's carriage drove off, and the gentleman
who had attended her walked back with a satisfied
air into the house for his overcoat, and possibly his
cigar-case.   As he hurried in, he was fastening a
white rose in his button-hole.   A sister flower,
drooping and fading, perhaps from nearer contact
with its late owner, lay unnoticed on the pavement.
I have seen so many of these vegetables exchanged,

particularly towards the close of an entertainment,
that I took little notice either of the keepsake, precious and perishable, or its discarded companion; but
I remember now to have heard in clubs and other
places of resort, how pale beautiful Mrs. Vandeleur
went by the name of the White Rose; a title none
the less appropriate, that she was supposed to be
plentifully girt with thorns, and that many well-
known fingers were said to have been pricked to the
bone in their efforts to detach her from her stem.

There is a philosophy in most men towards five in
the morning, supposing them to have been up all
night, which tends to an idle contemplation of
human nature, and indulgent forbearance towards
its weaknesses. I generally encourage this frame
of mind by the thoughtful consumption of a cigar.
Turning round to light one, a few paces from Lady
Billesdon's door, I was startled to observe a shab-
bily-dressed figure advance stealthily from the
corner of the street, where it seemed to have been
on the watch, and pounce at the withered rose,
crushed and yellowing on the pavement. As it
passed swiftly by me, I noticed the figure was that
of a man in the prime of life, but in bad health
and apparently narrow circumstances. His hair

was matted, his face pale, and his worn-out clothes
hung loosely from the angles of his frame. He took
no heed of my presence, was probably unconscious
of it ; for I perceived his eyes fill with tears as he
pressed the crushed flower passionately to his lips
and heart, muttering in broken sentences the while.

I only caught the words, " I have seen you once
more, my darling! I swore I would, and it is worth
it all !" Then his strength gave way, for he stopped
and leaned his head against the area railings of the
street. I could see, by the heaving of his shoulders,
the man was sobbing like a child. Uncertain how
to act, ere I could approach nearer he had recovered
himself and was gone.

Could this be _her_ doing ? Was Norah Vandeleur
indeed a witch, and was nobody to be exempt from
her spells ? Was she to send home the sleek child
of fortune, pleased with the superfluity of a flower
and a flirtation too much, while she could not even
spare the poor emaciated wretch who had darted on
the withered rose she dropped with the avidity of a
famished hawk on its prey? What could he be,
this man ? and what connection could possibly exist
between him and handsome, high-bred Mrs. Vandeleur ?

All these things I learned afterwards, partly from my own observation, partly from the confessions of those concerned. Adding to my early recollections of Norah Welby the circumstances that came to my knowledge both before and after she changed her name to Vandeleur, I am enabled to tell my tale, such as it is ; and I can think of no more appropriate title for the story of a fair and suffering woman than " The White Rose."

CHAPTER II.

ON a fine sunshiny morning, not very many years ago, two boys—I beg their pardon, two young gentlemen—were sitting in the comfortless pupil-room of a "retired officer and graduate of Cambridge," undergoing the process of being "crammed." The retired officer and graduate of Cambridge had disappeared for luncheon, and the two young gentlemen immediately laid aside their books to engage in an animated discussion totally unconnected with their previous studies. It seemed such a relief to unbend the mind after an hour's continuous attention to any subject whatever, that they availed themselves of the welcome relaxation without delay. I am bound to admit their conversation was instructive in the least possible degree.

"I say, Gerard," began the elder of the two, "what's become of Dandy? He was off directly after breakfast, and to-day's his day for 'General Information.' I wonder 'Nobs' stood it, but he lets Dandy do as he likes."

"Nobs," be it observed, was the term of respect by which Mr. Archer was known among his pupils.

"Nobs is an old muff, and Dandy's a swell," answered Gerard, who had tilted his chair on its hind-legs against the wall for the greater convenience of shooting paper-spills at the clock. "I shall be off, too, as soon as I have finished these equations; and I'm afraid, Dolly, you'll have to spend another afternoon by yourself."

He spoke nervously, and stooped so low to pick one of the spills, that it seemed to bring all the blood in his body to his face; but his blushes were lost on Dolly, who looked out of window, and answered tranquilly—

"Like all great men, Gerard, I am never so little alone as when alone—'My mind to me a thingamy is!' You two fellows have no resources within yourselves. Now I shall slope easily down to the mill, lift the trimmers, smoke a weed with old 'Grits,' and wile away the pleasant afternoon with a

pot of mild porter;—peradventure, if Grits is
thirsty—of which I make small doubt—we shall
accomplish two. And where may you be going,
Master Jerry, this piping afternoon? Not across
the marshes again, my boy. You've been there
twice already this week."

Once more Gerard blushed like a girl, and this
time without escaping the observation of his companion ; nor was his confusion lessened by the good-
humoured malice with which the latter began to
sing in a full mellow voice—

> " Sho hath an eye so soft and brown—
>   ' Ware, hare !
> She gives a side glance, and looks down—
>   ' Ware, hare !

Master Jerry, she's fooling thee ! "

Dolly, whose real name nobody ever called him
by, enjoyed a great talent for misquotation, and a
tendency to regard life in general from its ludicrous
point of view. Otherwise, he was chiefly remarkable for a fat, jovial face ; a person to correspond ;
strong absorbing and digestive faculties ; a good
humour that nothing could ruffle ; and an extraordi-
nary facility in dismissing useful information from his
mind. He was heir to a sufficient fortune, and, if he

could pass his examination, his friends intended he should become a Hussar.

Mr. Archer was at this period employed in the preparation of three young gentlemen for the service of her Majesty. Military examinations were then in an early stage of development, but created, nevertheless, strong misgivings in the minds of parents and guardians, not to mention the extreme disgust with which they were viewed by future heroes indisposed to book-learning. It was a great object to find an instructor who could put the required amount of information into a pupil's head in the shortest possible space of time, without reference to its stay there after an examination had been passed, and Mr. Archer was notorious for his success in this branch of tuition. Clever or stupid, idle or industrious, with him it was simply a question of weeks.

"I will put your young gentleman through the mill," he would observe to an anxious father or an over-sanguine mamma ; "but whether it takes him three months or six, or a whole year, depends very much upon himself. Natural abilities ! there's no such thing ! If he will learn, he *shall*; if he won't, he *must* ! "

So Mr. Archer's three small bed-rooms, with

their white furniture and scanty carpets, never wanted occupants; the bare, comfortless pupil-room, with its dirty walls and dingy ceiling, never remained empty; and Mr. Archer himself, who was really a clever man, found his banker's account increasing in proportion to his own disgust for history, classics, geometry, engineering—all that had once afforded him a true scholar's delight. It speaks well for learning, and the spells she casts over her lovers, that they can never quite free themselves from her fascinations. Even the over-worked usher of a grammar-school needs but a few weeks' rest to return to his allegiance, and to glory once more in the stern mistress he adores. Mr. Archer, after a few months' vacation, could perhaps take pride and pleasure in the cultivation of his intellect; but at the end of his half year, jaded, disgusted, and over-worked, he could have found it in his heart to envy the very day-labourer mowing his lawn.

That this military Mentor had enough on his hands may be gathered from the following summary of his pupils :—

First. Granville Burton, a young gentleman of prepossessing appearance, and a florid taste in dress. Antecedents: Eton; two ponies, a servant of his own at sixteen, and a mother who had spoilt him from the day he was born. Handsome, fatherless, and heir to a good property, ever since he could remember he had been nicknamed " Dandy," and was intended for the Life-Guards.

Secondly. Charles Egremont, commonly called Dolly, already described.

Lastly. Gerard Ainslie, one of those young gentlemen of whom it is so difficult to predict the future —a lad in years, a man in energy, but almost a woman in feelings. Gifted, indeed, with a woman's quick perceptions and instinctive sense of right, but cursed with her keen affections, her vivid fancy, and painful tendencies to self-torture and self-immolation. Such a character is pretty sure to be popular both with men and boys, also, perhaps, with the other sex. Young Ainslie, having his own way to make in the world, often boasted that he always " lit on his legs."

An orphan, and dependent on a great-uncle whom he seldom saw, the army was indeed to be his profession ; and to him, far more than either of the others, it was important that he should go up for his examinations with certainty of success. It is needless to observe that he was the idlest of the three. By fits and starts he would take it into his head to work hard for a week at a time—"Going in for a grind," as he called it—with a vigour and determination that astonished Mr. Archer himself.

"Ainslie," observed that gentleman after one of these efforts, in which his pupil had done twice the usual tasks in half the usual time, "there are two sorts of fools—the fool positive, who can't help himself, and the fool superlative, who won't! You make me think you belong to the latter class. If you would only exert yourself, you might pass in a month from this time."

"I can work, sir, well enough," replied the pupil, "when I have an object."

"An object!" retorted the tutor, lifting his eyebrows in that stage of astonishment which is but one degree removed from disgust; "gracious heavens, sir, if your whole success in life, your character, your position, the very bread you eat, is not an object, I should like to know what is!"

Gerard knew, but he wasn't going to tell Mr. Archer; and I think that in this instance the latter showed less than his usual tact and discrimination in the characters of the young.

It was in pursuit of this object no doubt that Gerard finished his equations so rapidly and put his books on the shelf with a nervous eagerness that denoted more than common excitement, to which Dolly's imperturbable demeanour afforded a wholesome contrast.

"Off again, Jerry," observed the latter, still intent on a mathematical figure requiring the construction of a square and a circle, on which he lavished much unnecessary accuracy and neatness, to the utter disregard of the demonstration it involved; "I envy you, my boy—and yet I would not change places with you after all. You'll have a pleasant journey, like the cove in the poem—

> All in the blue unclouded weather,
> Thick-jewelled shone the saddle-leather,
> The helmet and the helmet feather
> Burnt like one burning flame together,
>   As he rode down to Camelot,
>   'Tirra-lirra! It's deuced hot,'
>   Sang Sir Launcelot.

—That's what I call real poetry, Jerry. I say, I met Tennyson once at my old governor's. He didn't jaw much. I thought him rather a good chap. You've got three miles of it across those blazing marshes.

I'll take odds you don't do it in thirty-five minutes
—walking, of course, heel and toe."

"Bother!" replied Jerry, and, snatching his hat
from its peg, laid his hand on the open window-sill,
vaulted through, and was gone.

Dolly returned to his problem, shaking his head
with considerable gravity.

"Now, that young chap will come to grief," he
soliloquised. "He wants looking after, and who's
to look after him? If it was Dandy Burton I
shouldn't so much mind. The Dandy can take
precious good care of himself. What he likes is
to 'get up' awful, and be admired. Wouldn't he
just—

> Stand at his diamond-door,
> With his rainbow-frill unfurled,
> And swear if he was uncurled?

Now Jerry's different. Jerry's a good sort, and I
don't want to see the young beggar go a mucker
for want of a little attention. Grits is a sensible
chap enough—I never knew a miller that wasn't.
I'll just drop easily down the lane and talk it over
with Grits."

In pursuance of which discreet resolution, Dolly
—who, although actually the junior, believed him-

self in wisdom and general experience many years older than his friend—sauntered out into the sunshine with such deliberation that ere he had gone a hundred yards, the other, speeding along as if he trod on air, was already more than half through his journey.

And he *was* treading on air. The long, level marshes through which he passed, with their straight banks, their glistening ditches, their wet, luxuriant herbage and hideous pollard willows, would have seemed to you or me but a flat uninteresting landscape, to be tolerated only for the stock it could carry and the remunerative interest it paid on the capital sunk in drainage per acre; but to Gerard Ainslie it was simply fairy-land—the fairy-land through which most of us pass, if only for a few paces, at some period of our lives. Few enter it more than once, for we remember when we emerged how cold it was outside; we shudder when we think of the bleak wind that buffeted our bodies and chilled our quivering hearts; we have not forgotten how long it took to harden us for our bleak native atmosphere, and we dare not risk so sad a change again!

The marshes, whether fairy-land or pasture, soon disappeared beneath Gerard's light and active footfall. What is a mere league of distance to a well-made lad of nineteen—a runner, a leaper, a cricketer—tolerably in condition, and, above all, very much in love? He was soon in a wooded district, amongst deep lanes, winding footpaths, thick hedges, frequent stiles, and a profusion of wild flowers. He threaded his way as if he knew it well. Presently the colour faded from his cheek and his heart began to beat, for he had reached a wicket-gate in a high, mouldering, ivy-grown wall, and beyond it he knew was a smooth-shaven lawn, a spreading cypress, a wealth of roses, and the prettiest parsonage within four counties. He had learnt the trick of the gate, and had opened it often enough, yet he paused for a moment outside. Although he had walked his three miles pretty fast, he had been perfectly cool hitherto, but now he drew his handkerchief across his face, while, with white parched lips and trembling fingers, he turned the handle of the wicket and passed through.

CHAPTER III.

NORAH.

THE lawn, the cedar, the roses, there they were exactly as he had pictured them to himself last night in his dreams, that morning when he awoke, the whole forenoon in the dreary study, through those eternal equations. Nothing was wanting, not even the low chair, the slender work-table, nor the presence that made a paradise of it all.

She was sitting in a white dress beneath the drooping lime-tree that gleamed and quivered in the sunbeams, alive with its hum of insects, heavy in its wealth of summer fragrance, and raining its shower of blossoms with every breath that whispered through its leaves. For many a year after, perhaps his whole life long, he never forgot her as she sat before him then; never forgot the gold on her rich

chestnut hair, the light in her deep fond eyes, nor
the tremble of happiness in her voice, while she
exclaimed, "Gerard! And again to-day! How did
you manage to come over? It is so late I had almost
given you up!"

She had half-risen, as if her impulse was to rush
towards him, but sat down again, and resumed her
work with tolerable composure, though parted lips
and flushing cheek betrayed only too clearly how
welcome was this intrusion on her solitude.

He was little more than nineteen, and he loved
her very dearly. He could find nothing better to
say than this: "I only wanted to bring you some
music. The others are engaged, and I had really
nothing else to do. How is Mr. Welby?"

"Papa was quite well," she answered, demurely
enough, "and very busy, as usual at this hour, in
his own den. Should she let him know,"—and
there was a gleam of mirth in her eye, a suspicion
of malice in her tone,—"should she run and tell
him Mr. Ainslie was here?"

"By no means," answered Gerard, needlessly
alarmed at such a suggestion; "I would not disturb him on any consideration. And, Norah!—you
said I might call you Norah at the Archery
Meeting."

"Did I?" replied the young lady, looking exceedingly pretty and provoking; "I can't have
meant it if I did."

"Oh, Norah!" he interposed, reproachfully, "you
don't mean to say you've forgotten!"

"I haven't forgotten that you were extremely
cross, and ate no luncheon, and behaved very badly,"
she answered, laughing. "Never mind, Gerard, we
made friends coming home, didn't we? And if I
said you might, I suppose you must. Now you
look all right again, so don't be a rude boy, but
tell me honestly if you walked all this way in
the sun only because you had nothing better to
do?"

His eyes glistened. "You know why I come
here," he said. "You know why I would walk a
thousand miles barefoot to see you for five minutes.
Now I shall be contented all to-day and to-morrow,
and then next morning I shall begin to get restless and anxious, and if I can, I shall come here
again."

"You dear fidget!" she answered, with a bright
smile. "I know I can believe you, and it makes me
very happy. Now hold these silks while I wind
them; and after that, if you do it well, I'll give you

some tea; and then you shall see papa, who is really
very fond of you, before you go back."

So the two sat down—in fairy-land—under the
lime-tree, to wind silks—a process requiring little
physical exertion, and no great effort of mind. It
seemed to engross their whole energies nevertheless,
and to involve a good deal of conversation, carried
on in a very low tone. I can guess almost all they
said, but should not repeat such arrant nonsense,
even had I overheard every syllable. It was only
that old story, I suppose, the oldest of all, but to
which people never get tired of listening; and
the sameness of which in every language, and
under all circumstances, is as remarkable as its
utter want of argument, continuity, or common
sense.

Gerard Ainslie and Miss Welby had now known
each other for about six months, a sufficiently long
period to allow of very destructive campaigns both
in love and war. They had fallen in love, as people
call it, very soon after their first introduction, that
is to say, they had thought about each other a good
deal, met often enough to keep up a vivid recollection
of mutual sayings and doings, yet with sufficient
uncertainty to create constant excitement, none the

less keen for frequent disappointments; and, in
short, had gone through the usual probation by
which that accident of an accident, an unwise
attachment between two individuals, becomes
strengthened in exact proportion to its hopelessness,
its inconvenience, and the undoubted absurdity that
it should exist at all.

People said Mr. Welby encouraged it; whereas
poor Mr. Welby, who would have esteemed the
prince in a fairy tale not half good enough for his
daughter, was simply pleased to think that she
should have companions of her own age, male or
female, who could bring a brighter lustre to her eye,
a softer bloom to her cheek. It never occurred to
him for a moment that his Norah, his own peculiar
pride and pet and constant companion since he lost
her mother at four years old, should dream of caring
for anybody but himself, at least for many a long
day to come. If he did contemplate such a possi-
bility, it was with a vague, misty idea that in some
ten years or so, when he was ready to drop into his
grave, some great nobleman would lay a heart, and
a coronet to match, at his child's feet, and under
the circumstances such an arrangement would be
exceedingly suitable for all concerned. But that

Norah, *his* Norah, should allow her affections to be
entangled by young Gerard Ainslie, though a prime
favourite of his own, why I do not believe such a
contingency could have been placed before him in
any light that could have caused him to admit the
remotest chance of its existence.

Nevertheless, while Mr. Welby was making bad
English of excellent Greek, under the impression
that he was rendering the exact meaning of Euripides for the benefit of unlearned men, his daughter
and her young adorer were enacting the old comedy,
tragedy, farce, or pantomime—for it partakes of the
nature of all these entertainments—on their own
little stage, with scenery, dresses, and decorations to
correspond.   Ah! we talk of eloquence, expression,
fine writing forsooth ! and the trick of word-painting,
as very a trick as any other turn of the handi-
craftsman's trade ; but who ever read in a whole
page of print one half the poetry condensed into two
lines of a woman's manuscript—ungrammatical, if
you please, ill expressed, and with long tails to the
letters, yet breathing in every syllable that sentiment of ideality which has made the whole orna-
mental literature of the world ?   After all, the head
only reproduces what the heart creates ; and so we

give the mocking-bird credit when he imitates the loving murmurs of the dove.

If oratory should be judged by its effect, then must Norah Welby and Gerard Ainslie have been speakers of the highest calibre. To be sure, they had already practised in a good many rehearsals, and ought to have been pretty well up in their parts.

The simultaneous start with which they increased their distance by at least a fathom, on hearing the door-bell jingling all over the house, would have ensured a round of applause from any audience in Europe.

"How provoking!" exclaimed the girl; "and people so seldom come here on a Tuesday. Perhaps, after all, it's only somebody for papa."

Gerard said nothing, but his colour deepened, and a frown of very obvious annoyance lowered on his brow. It did not clear the more to observe an open carriage, with a pair of good-looking horses, driven round to the stables. As paint and varnish glistened in the sunshine through the laurels, Miss Welby drew a long sigh of relief.

"It might have been worse," she said; "it might have been the Warings, all of them, with their aunt, or that dreadful Lady Baker, or Mrs. Brown; but it's only Mr. Vandeleur, and he won't stay long. Besides, he's always pleasant and good-natured, and never says the wrong thing. We won't have tea though till he's gone."

"It seems to me, Norah," answered her visitor, "that you rather like Mr. Vandeleur."

"Like him! I should think I did!" protested the young lady; "but you needn't look so fierce about it, Master Jerry. I like him because papa does; he's always in better spirits after a visit from Mr. Vandeleur. Besides, he's immensely clever you know, and well-read, and all that. Papa says he might be in the Government if he chose to go into Parliament. Not that I care about clever people myself; I think it's much nicer to be like you, Jerry, you stupid boy! I don't think you'll ever pass your examination—and so much the better, for then you won't have to go away, and leave us all, and—and forget us."

"Forget you!" replied Gerard, decreasing by one-half the distance he had taken up from his companion. What more he might have said was cut short by the appearance of a gentleman whose step had been unheard on the thick velvet turf, and who now came forward to greet his hostess, with an admirable mixture of the deference due to a young lady, and the cordiality permitted from an old friend.

" I came through the garden on purpose to say how d'ye do," he observed, with marked politeness, " but my visit is really to your father. I hope he is not too busy to see me for half-an-hour. In fact, I believe he expected me either to-day or to-morrow." Then turning to Gerard, he shook him warmly by the hand, and congratulated him on the score he had made a few days before in a cricket match.

Norah was right. Mr. Vandeleur was not a man to say the wrong thing, even under the most unfavourable circumstances. Those who knew him best affirmed that he was not to be hurried, nor taken aback, nor found at a loss. He would have been exceedingly popular, but that never for more than a few seconds could he look anybody in the face.

His eyes shifted uneasily from Gerard's even now. The latter did not like him, and though he answered civilly, was too young to conceal his aversion ; but Vandeleur, with all the advantage of position, manner, and experience, still more of the man over

the boy, and, above all, of the careless admirer over
the devoted slave, felt too safe not to be in good
humour, and put in even for Gerard's approval by
the tact with which he veiled his consciousness of
intrusion, while he announced his intention to
withdraw.

" I see you have both more work to do," he observed, gaily pointing to a skein of silk that still
hung over the back of Norah's chair, for in truth
the operation had been going on very slowly, " and
I have, as usual, a thousand things to attend to
between this and dinner. Miss Welby, do you think
I might venture to invade your father at once in
his study? If you are not gone in half-an-hour,
Ainslie, I can give you a lift most of the way back.
I should like you to get your hand on those chestnuts of mine. The white-legged one is the only
perfect phaeton-horse I ever had in my life. I will
come and make my bow to Miss Welby before I
start."

" Isn't he nice?" exclaimed Norah, as the visitor
disappeared under the low ivy-grown porch of the
Parsonage. " He always seems to do exactly what
you want without finding you out. And if you're
tired or stupid, or don't like to talk, he'll neither

bore you himself nor let other people worry you.
Isn't he nice, I say? Master Jerry, why can't you
answer? Don't you know that I will insist on your
liking everybody I like?"

"I cannot like Mr. Vandeleur," answered Gerard
doggedly, for not even the compliment implied in
asking his opinion of the phaeton-horses—a compliment generally so acceptable at nineteen—had over-
come his distaste to this gentleman. "I never *did*
like him, and I never *shall* like him. And I think
I hate him all the more, Norah, because—because———"

"Because what?" asked Miss Norah, pettishly;
"because *I* like him?"

"Because I think he likes you," answered Gerard,
with a very red face; adding somewhat injudiciously,
"it's absurd, it's ridiculous! An old man like that!"

"He's not so very old," observed the young lady,
maliciously; "and he's tolerably good-looking still."

"He's a widower, at any rate," urged Gerard;
"and they say he regularly killed his first
wife."

"So did Bluebeard," replied wicked Miss Norah;
"and look how people made up to him afterwards!
Do you know, I don't see why Mr. Vandeleur

shouldn't settle down into a very good husband for anybody."

Gerard had been red before ; he turned pale now.

" Do you really mean that ? " he asked in tones rather lower and more distinct than common.

" For anybody of his own age, of course," answered the provoking girl. " Not for a *young* lady, you know. Why, he must be very nearly as old as papa. I wish he'd come to say ' Good-bye ' all the same, though he must take you with him. Poor boy ! you'll never get back in time, and you'll be so hot if you have to run all the way."

Even while she spoke, a servant came out of the Parsonage with a message. It was to give " Mr. Vandeleur's compliments, and one of his horses had lost a shoe. He feared to make Mr. Ainslie too late, if he waited till it was put on."

" And you've never had your tea after all ! " exclaimed Norah, about to recall the servant and order that beverage forthwith.

But Ainslie did not want any tea, and could not stay for it if he had wanted some. Even his light foot could hardly be expected to do the three miles much under twenty-five minutes, and he must be off at once. He hated going, and she hated parting

with him. Probably they told each other so, for the
servant was already out of hearing, and his back
was turned.

We may follow the servant's example. We have
no wish to be spies on the leave-taking of two young
lovers at nineteen.

CHAPTER IV.

I HAVE not the slightest doubt the chestnut horse's shoe was off when he arrived, and that his owner was perfectly aware of the loss while so politely offering Gerard Ainslie a lift back in his carriage, but Mr. Vandeleur was a gentleman untroubled by scruples either in small things or great. His principle, if he had any, was never to practise insincerity unless it was necessary, or at least extremely convenient, except where women were concerned; in such cases he considered deceit not only essential, but praiseworthy. As a young man, Vandeleur had been a profligate, when open profligacy was more the fashion than at present; while good looks, a good constitution, and a good fortune, helped him to play his part successfully enough on the stage of life, in

London or Paris, as the pleasant, popular good-for-
nothing, who in spite of his extravagance was never
out-at-elbows, in spite of his excesses was never out
of spirits or out of humour. With a comely exterior,
a healthy digestion, and a balance at his banker's, a
man requires but few sterling qualities to make his
way in a society that troubles itself very little about
its neighbours so long as they render themselves
agreeable, in a world that while not entirely averse
to being shocked, is chiefly intolerant of being
bored.

Some of those who ministered to his pleasures
might indeed have told strange stories about Vandeleur, and one violent scene in Paris was only hushed
up by the tact of an exalted foreign friend, and
the complicity of a *sergent de ville ;* but such trifling
matters were below the surface, and in no way
affected his popularity, particularly amongst the
ladies, with whom a little mystery goes a long
way, and into whose good graces the best initiative
step is to awaken a curiosity, that seldom fails to
chafe itself into interest if left for a time un-
gratified. It can only have been some morbid
desire to learn more of him at all risks, that tempted
the daughter of a ducal house to trust her life's

happiness in so frail a bark as that of Vandeleur.
"Lady Margaret must be a bold girl!" was the
general opinion expressed at White's, Boodle's, and
Arthur's, in the boudoirs of Belgravia, and the
dining-rooms of Mayfair, when her marriage was
announced, and it was observed that the bridegroom's intimate friends were those who showed most
disapprobation of the alliance, and who chiefly com-
miserated the bride. Nevertheless, bold or blushing,
Lady Margaret married him decorously, attended
the wedding-breakfast afterwards, and eventually
drove off in a very becoming lilac travelling-dress
to spend the honeymoon at Oakover, her husband's
old family place. But she never came back to
London. For two years husband and wife disappeared entirely from the set in which they had
hitherto lived, regretted loudly, missed but little,
as is the way of the world. They travelled a good
deal, they vegetated at their country place, but at
home or abroad never seemed to be an hour apart.

Some people said she was jealous, frightfully
jealous, and would not let him out of her sight;
some that they were a most attached couple; some
that Lady Margaret's health had grown very pre-
carious, and she required constant attention. Her

own family shook their heads and agreed, "Margaret was much altered since her marriage, and seemed so wrapped up in her husband that she had quite forgotten her own relations. As for him—Well, they didn't know what she had done to him, but he certainly used to be much pleasanter as a bachelor!"

Lady Margaret had no children, yet she lost her looks day by day. At the end of two years the blinds were down at Oakover, and its mistress was lying dead in the bed-room that had been decorated so beautifully to receive her as a bride. The sun rose and set more than once before Vandeleur could be persuaded to leave her body. A belated housemaid, creeping upstairs to bed, frightened out of her wits at any rate by the bare idea of a death in the house, heard his laughter ringing wild and shrill in that desolate chamber at the end of the corridor. Long afterwards, in her next place, the poor girl would wake up in the night, terrified by the memory of that fearful mirth, which haunted even her dreams. On the day of Lady Margaret's funeral, however, the mourners were surprised to see how bravely her husband bore his loss. In a few weeks, the same people declared themselves shocked to hear that Mr. Vandeleur went about much as usual; in a few months, were surprised to learn he had retired from the world and gone into a monastery.

The monastery turned out to be simply a yacht of considerable tonnage. For two years Vandeleur absented himself from England, and of that two years he either would not, or could not, give any account. When he returned, the ladies would have made him a second Lara, had he shown the least tendency to the mysterious and romantic; but he turned up one morning in Hyde Park as if nothing had happened, paid his penny for a chair, lit his cigar, took his hat off to the smartest ladies with his old manner, went to the Opera, and in twenty-four hours was as thoroughly re-established in London as if he had never married, and never left it.

He was still rather good-looking, but affected a style of dress and deportment belonging to a more advanced period of life than he had attained. His hair and whiskers were grizzled, indeed, and there were undoubted wrinkles about his keen restless eyes, as on his healthy, weather-browned cheek; yet none of the ladies voted him too old to marry; they even

protested he was not too old to dance; and I believe
that at no period of his life would Vandeleur have
had a better chance of winning a nice wife than in
the first season after his return from his mysterious
disappearance.

He did not seem the least inclined to take advantage of his luck. While at Oakover, indeed, he
busied himself to a certain extent with a country
gentleman's duties and amusements—attended magis-
trates' meetings at rare intervals, asked a houseful of
neighbours to shoot, dine, and sleep, two or three
times during the winter; was present at one archery
meeting in October, and expressed an intention he
did not fulfil, of going to the County Ball; but in
London he appeared to relapse insensibly into his
bachelor ways and bachelor life, so that the Vandeleur of forty was, I fear, little more useful or respectable a member of society than the Vandeleur of
twenty-five.

A few years of such a life, and the proprietor of
Oakover seemed to have settled down into a regular
groove of refined self-indulgence. The tongue of
scandal wags so freely when it has once been set
going, that no wonder it soon tires itself out, and a
man who pays lavishly for his pleasures finds it a

long time before they rise up in judgment against
him. Even in a country neighbourhood it is possible
to establish a prescriptive right for doing wrong;
and while the domestic arrangements at Oakover
itself were conducted with the utmost decorum and
propriety, people soon ceased to trouble themselves
about its master's doings when out of his own house.

For an idle man Vandeleur was no mean scholar.
The sixth form at Eton, and a good degree at
Oxford, had not cured him of a taste for classic
literature, and he certainly did derive a pleasure
from his visits to Mr. Welby's Parsonage, which
had nothing to do with the bright eyes of the
clergyman's daughter.

Host and guest had much in common. Welby
himself, before he entered the Church—of which it
is but fair to say he was a conscientious minister—
had been familiar, so to speak, with the ranks of the
Opposition. Even now he looked back to the bril-
liancy of that pleasant, wicked world, as the crew of
Ulysses may have recalled the wild delights of their
enchanted island. False they were, no doubt—
lawless, injurious, debasing; yet tinged, they felt too
keenly, with an unearthly gleam of joy from heaven
or hell. They are thankful to have escaped, yet

would they not forego the strange experience if they could.

Miss Welby was right when she said her father always seemed in better spirits after a visit from Mr. Vandeleur; perhaps that was why she received the latter so graciously when, emerging from the study, he crossed the lawn to take leave of her some twenty minutes after Gerard Ainslie's departure.

He ought to have been no bad judge, and he thought he had never seen a woman look so well. Happiness is a rare cosmetic; and though, as many a man had reason to admit, sorrow in after years refined, idealised, and gave a more elevated character to her beauty, I doubt if Norah was ever more captivating to Vandeleur than on that bright summer's afternoon under the lime-trees.

She was thinking of Gerard, as a woman thinks of her idol for the time. That period may be a lifetime, or it may last only for a year or two, or for a few months. I have even heard three weeks specified as its most convenient duration; but long or short, no doubt the worship is sincere and engrossing while it exists. The little flutter, the subdued agitation created by the presence of her lover, had vanished, but the feeling of intense happiness, the

sense of complete dependence and repose, steeped her
in an atmosphere of security and contentment that
seemed to glorify her whole being, and to enhance
even the physical superiority of her charms. She
felt so thankful, so joyful, so capable of everything
that was noble or good, so completely in charity
with all the world! No wonder she greeted her
father's friend with a cordial manner and a bright
smile.

"Your carriage has not come round yet, Mr.
Vandeleur," she said, "and they will bring tea in
five minutes. Papa generally comes out and has a
cup with us here. You at least are not obliged to
hurry away," she added rather wistfully, glancing
at the chair which Gerard had lately occupied.

His eye followed hers. "I am glad I'm too old
for a private tutor," he answered with a meaning
smile. "That's a very nice boy, Miss Welby, that
young Mr. Ainslie; and how sorry he seemed to go
away."

She blushed. It was embarrassing to talk about
Gerard, but still it was not unpleasant.

"We all like him very much," she said guardedly,
meaning probably by "all," herself, her papa, and
her bullfinch, which comprised the family.

"A nice gentleman-like boy," continued Mr. Vandeleur; "well-disposed, too, I can see. When I was his age, Miss Welby, I don't think I should have been so amenable to discipline under the same temptation. I fancy my tutor might have whistled for me, if I wanted to be late for dinner. Ah! we were wilder in my time, and most of us have turned out badly in consequence; but I like this lad, I assure you, very much. None the less that he seems so devoted to you. Have you known him long?"

Luckily the tea had just arrived, and Norah could bend her blushing face over the cups.

Had she known Gerard long? Well, it seemed so; and yet the time had passed only too quickly. She had known him scarcely six months. Was that a long or a short acquaintance in which to have become so fond of him?

With faltering voice she replied, " Yes—no—not very long—ever since last winter, when he came to Mr. Archer's."

" Who is he? and what is he?" continued Vandeleur, sipping his tea calmly. " Do they mean him for a soldier? Will my friend Archer make anything of him? Don't you pity poor Archer, Miss Welby? A scholar, a gentleman, a fellow who has

seen some service, and might have distinguished
himself if he had stuck to the army. And now he
is condemned to spend seven hours a day in licking
cubs into shape for inspection by the Horse Guards."

"There are no *cubs* there this year," she answered
with some spirit. "Mr. Burton, and Mr. Egremont,
and the rest, are very gentleman-like, pleasant
young men, and just as clever as anybody else!"

"That is not saying much," he replied, with perfect good humour; "but when I talk of 'cubs' I
declare to you I don't mean your friend and mine,
Mr. Ainslie. I tell you I have taken a great fancy
to the boy, and would do him a turn if I could. I
suppose he would like to get his commission at
once?"

Even at nineteen she was yet woman enough to
have studied his future welfare; and his "getting
his commission" was the point to which she had so
often looked forward with dismay as the termination
of their happiness—it might be, something whispered
to her ominously, even of their friendship. Nevertheless, she knew it would be for his advantage to
enter the army at once. She knew he was wasting
his time here, in nothing perhaps more than in his
oft-repeated visits to herself. Her heart sank when

she thought of the lawn, and the cedar, and the lime-trees, without those visits to look back on, and look forward to, but she answered bravely, though her face turned very pale—

"Certainly! It would be of great importance to Mr. Ainslie, I believe; and I am sure he would be grateful to anybody who could help him to it."

She would have added, "And so should I," but a sensation as if she were choking stopped her short.

"If you are interested about him, that is enough," replied Vandeleur. "I will try what can be done, and small as is my interest, it ought to be sufficient to carry out so very common-place a job as this. In the meantime what a hot walk the poor boy will have! I wish he could have waited, I would have driven him to Archer's door. It's a good thing to be young, Miss Welby, but no doubt there are certain disadvantages connected with a prosperity that is still *to come*. In ten years that young gentleman will be a rising man, I venture to predict. In twenty a successful one, with a position and a name in the world. Twenty years! It's a long time, isn't it? I shall be in my grave, and you— why even you will have left off being a young lady then."

She was thinking the same herself. Would it really be twenty years before poor Gerard could reach the lowest round of that ladder on which she longed to see him? Mr. Vandeleur had great experience, he must know best, he was a thorough man of the world. What an unfair world it was. Poor Gerard!

She sighed, and raising her eyes to her companion's face, who instantly looked away, was conscious he had read her thoughts: this added to her discomposure, and for the moment she felt as if she could cry. Vandeleur knew every turn of the game he was playing, and saw that for the present he had better enact any part than that of confidant. Later, perhaps, when Gerard was gone, and the blank required filling up, it might be judicious to assume that, or any other character, which would give him access to her society; but at the present stage, disinterested friendship was obviously the card to play, and he produced it without hesitation.

"Then that is settled!" he said gaily. "I'll do what I can, and if I don't succeed you may be sure it's not for want of good-will to you and yours. I'm an old friend, you know, Miss Welby—if not of your own, at least of your father's; and believe me, it would be a great pleasure to serve you in anything. Anything!—a caprice, a fancy, what you will. Black or white, right or wrong, easy or difficult—*or impossible.* That's plain speaking, isn't it? I don't do things by halves! And now I must really be off; those horses of mine have pawed a regular pit in your gravel-walk, and half-a-dozen country neighbours are waiting dinner for me at this moment, I do believe. Good-bye, Miss Welby; keep your spirits up, and let me come and see you again when I've some good news to tell."

Still talking, he hurried away, and drove off at a gallop, waving his whip cheerfully above the laurels as he passed within sight of the lawn. Norah thought she had never liked him so much as when the grating of his wheels died out in the stillness of the summer evening, and she was left alone with her own thoughts.

CHAPTER V.

THE MAID OF THE MILL.

Mr. Vandeleur always drove fast. He liked to know that the poor countryman breaking stones on the road, or laying the fence by its side, looked after him as he flashed by, with stolid admiration on his dull face, and muttered, "Ah! there goes Squire Vandeleur, surelie!" On the present occasion his pace was even better than common, and the chestnuts laid themselves down to their work in a form that showed the two hundred guineas a-piece he had paid for them was not a shilling too much. He pulled them back on their haunches, however, at a turn in the road, with a sudden energy that jerked his groom's chin against the rail of the driving-seat, and stopped his carriage within three feet of a showily-dressed young woman, who was gathering wild-flowers off the hedge with a transparent affectation of unconsciousness that she was observed.

"Why, Fanny," said he, leaning out of the carriage to look under her bonnet, "Fanny Draper, I thought you were in London, or Paris, at least;— or gone to the devil before your time," he added, in an undertone, between his teeth.

The lady thus accosted put her hand to her side with a faint catching of the breath, as of one in weak health, whose nerves are unequal to a shock. She glanced up at him from under her eye-lashes roguishly enough, however, while she replied—

"My! If it isn't Squire Vandeleur! I'm sure I never thought as you'd be the first person to meet me at my home-coming, and that's the truth." Here she dropped a saucy little curtsey. "I hope you've kept your health, sir, since I see you last!"

"Much you care for that, you little devil!" replied Vandeleur, with a familiar laugh. "My health is pretty good for an old one, and you look as handsome and as wicked as you ever did. So we needn't pay each other any more unmeaning compliments. Here! I've got something to say to you. Jump up, and I'll give you a lift home to the mill."

The girl's eyes sparkled, but she looked meaningly towards the groom at the horses' heads, and back in his master's face.

"Oh, never mind him!" exclaimed the latter, understanding the glance. "If my servants don't attend to their own business, at least they never trouble themselves about mine. Jump up, I tell you, and don't keep that off-horse fretting all night."·

She still demurred, though with an obvious intention of yielding at last.

"Suppose we should meet any of the neighbours, Mr. Vandeleur, or some of the gentlefolks coming home from the archery. Why, whatever would they think of you and me?"

"Please yourself," he answered, carelessly. "Only it's a long two miles to the mill, and I suppose you don't want to wear those pretty little boots out faster than you can help. Come! that's a good girl. I thought you would. Sit tight now. Never mind your dress. I'll tuck it in under the apron. Let 'em alone, Tom! And off she goes again!"

While he spoke, he stretched out his hand and helped her into the front seat by his side, taking especial care of the gaudy muslin skirt she wore. One word of encouragement was enough to make his horses dash freely at their collars, the groom jumped into his place like a harlequin, and the phaeton was again bowling through the still summer evening at the rate of twelve miles an hour.

When a tolerably popular person has earned a reputation for eccentricity, there is no end to the strange things he may do without provoking the censure, or even the comments, of his neighbours. Even had it not been the hour at which most of them were dressing for dinner, there was little likelihood that Vandeleur would meet any of his friends in the lonely road that skirted his property, ere it brought him to the confines of his park; but it is probable that even the most censorious, observing him driving a smartly-dressed person of the other sex in a lower grade of society than his own, would have made no more disparaging remark than that "Vandeleur was such a queer fellow, you never knew exactly what he was at!" He drove on, therefore, in perfect confidence, conversing very earnestly with his companion, though in such low tones that Tom's sharp ears in the back seat could scarcely make out a syllable he said. She listened attentively enough; more so, perhaps, than he had any right to expect, considering that her thoughts were distracted by the enviable situation in which she found herself,— driving in a real phaeton, by the side of a real gentleman, with a real servant in livery behind.

Fanny Draper had occupied from her youth a

position little calculated to improve either her good conduct or her good sense. She had been a village beauty almost as long as she could remember—ever since the time when she first began to do up her back-hair with a comb. The boys who sung in the choir made love to her when she went to the Sunday-school; the young farmers paid her devoted attention and quarrelled about her among themselves, the first day she ever attended a merry-making. She might have married a master-bricklayer at eighteen; and by the time she went out to service, was as finished a coquette in her own way as if she had been a French Marquise at the Court of Louis Quatorze.

Of course, to use the master-bricklayer's expression, such a "choice piece of goods" as the miller's daughter was above doing rough work, and the only situation she could think of taking was that of a lady's-maid; equally of course, she did not keep her first place three months, but returned to her father's mill before the expiration of that period, with rings on her fingers, a large stock of new clothes, and a considerable accession of self-esteem. Also, it is needless to add, like all lady's-maids, under a solemn engagement to be married to a butler!

Poor old Draper didn't know exactly what to

make of her. He had two sons doing well in his own business at the other end of England. He was a widower, Fanny was his only daughter, and the happiest day in the year to him was the one when she came home. Nevertheless, what with her watch, her rings, her white hands, her flowing dresses, and the number of followers she managed to collect about her even at the mill, the old man felt that she was too much for him, and that while she lived in it, the house never looked like his own. He admired her very much. He loved her very dearly. He seldom contradicted her; but he always smoked an extra pipe the night she went away, and yet he dreaded the time when she should make a sensible marriage (perhaps with the butler), and be "off his hands," as he expressed it, " for good and all."

Ripley Mill was but a little way from Oakover. It is not to be supposed that so comely a young woman as the miller's daughter escaped Mr. Vandeleur's observation. She took good care to throw herself in his way on every possible occasion, and the Squire, as her father called him, treated her with that sort of good-humoured, condescending, offensive familiarity, which, men seem to forget, is the worst possible compliment to any woman high

or low. That Miss Draper's vanity ever led her to
believe that she could captivate the Squire is more
than I will take upon me to assert, but no doubt it
was flattered by the trifling attentions he sometimes
paid her; and she had been heard to observe more
than once amongst her intimates, that "the Squire
was quite the gentleman, and let alone his appearance, which was neither here nor there, his manners
would always make him a prime favourite with the
ladies," invariably adding that, "for her part, the
Squire knew his place, and she knew hers."

The pace at which Vandeleur drove soon brought
them to a certain stile, over which Miss Fanny had
leant many a time in prolonged interviews with
different rustic lovers, and which was removed but
by one narrow orchard from her father's mill.
Short as was the time, however, the driver seemed
to have made the most of it, for his companion's
face looked flushed and agitated when she got down.
A perceptible shade of disappointment, and even
vexation, clouded her brow, while the voice in
which she bade him "Good evening," betrayed a
certain amount of pique and ill-humour bravely
kept under. Vandeleur's tone, on the contrary,
was confident and cheerful as usual.

"It's a bargain then," said he, releasing her hand, as she sprang on the foot-path from the top of the front wheel. " I can depend upon you, can't I ? to do your best or worst; and your worst with that pretty face of yours would tackle a much more difficult job than this. Honour, Miss Fanny! If you'll keep your word, you know I'll keep mine."

" Honour, Squire," replied she, with a forced smile that marred the comeliness of all the lower part of her face. " But you're in a desperate hurry! A week isn't much time, now, is it ? to finish a young gentleman right off."

" Those bright eyes of yours finished an old gentleman right off in a day," answered Vandeleur, laughing. "Good night, my dear, and stick to your bargain."

Before she was over the stile, his phaeton had turned a corner in the lane, and was out of sight.

Miss Draper took her bonnet off, and dangled it by the strings while the cool evening air breathed on her forehead and lifted her jetty locks. She was a pretty girl, no doubt, of a style by no means uncommon in her class. Dark eyes, high colour, irregular features, with a good deal of play in them,

a large laughing mouth, and a capital set of teeth,
made up a face that people turned round to look at
in market-places, or on high-roads, and her figure,
as she herself boasted, required "no making up,
with as little dressing as most people's, provided
only her things was good of their kind." Yes, she
was a handsome girl, and though her vanity had
received a considerable shock, she did not doubt it
even now.

After a few seconds' thought, her irritation seemed
to subside. Circumstances had for some years
forced Miss Draper's mind to take a practical turn.
Flattered vanity was a pleasing sensation, she
admitted, but tangible advantage was *the* thing
after all.

"Now whatever can the Squire be driving at?"
soliloquised his late companion, as threading the
apple-trees she came within hearing of the familiar
mill. "There's something behind all this, and
I'll be at the back of it as sure as my name's
Fanny! He's a deep 'un, is the Squire, but he's a
gentleman, I will say that! Quite the gentleman,
he is! Ten pounds down. Let me see, that will pay
for the two bonnets, and as much as I ever *will* pay
of Mrs. Markham's bill. And twenty more if it all

comes off right, within a month. Twenty pounds is a good deal of money! Yes, I always did uphold as the Squire were quite the gentleman."

She arrived simultaneously with this happy conclusion at the door of her paternal home, and the welcome of her father's professionally dusty embrace.

Vandeleur was not long in reaching Oakover, and commencing his toilet, which progressed rapidly, like everything else he did, without his appearing to hurry it. At a sufficiently advanced stage he rang for his valet. "Anybody come yet?" asked the host, tying a white neckcloth with the utmost precision.

"Sir Thomas Boulder, Colonel and Mrs. Waring, Lady Baker, Mrs. and Miss St. Denys, Major Blades, Captain Coverley, and Mr. Green," answered the well-drilled valet without faltering.

"Nobody else expected, is there?" was the next question, while his master pulled the bows to equal length.

"Dinner was ordered for ten, sir," answered his servant.

"Been here long?" asked Vandeleur, buttoning the watch-chain into his waistcoat.

"About three-quarters of an hour, sir," was the imperturbable reply.

"Very good. Then get dinner in five minutes!" and although nine hungry guests were waiting for him, Vandeleur employed that five minutes in writing a letter to a great nobleman, with whom he was on intimate terms.

While he ordered a man and horse to gallop off with it at once to the nearest post-town, in time for the night mail, he read the following lines over with a satisfied expression of countenance, and rather an evil smile.

"My DEAR LORD,—You can do me a favour, and I know I have only to ask it. I want a commission for a young friend of mind, as soon as ever it can be got. I believe he is quite ready for examination, or whatever you call the farce these young ones have to enact now-a-days. In *our* time people were not so particular about *anything*. Still I think you and I do pretty much as we like, and can't complain. On a slip of paper I enclose the young one's name and address. The sooner, for his own sake, we get him out of England the better,—and where he goes afterwards nobody cares a curse! You understand.

" Don't forget I expect you early next month, and will make sure there is a pleasant party to meet you.

" Ever yours,

"J. Vandeleur."

" Not a bad day's work altogether," muttered the writer as he stuck a stamp on the envelope, and went down to dinner.

CHAPTER VI.

IN pursuance of her bargain with Mr. Vandeleur, whatever it may have been, Fanny Draper attired herself in a very becoming dress after her one o'clock dinner on the following day, and proceeded to take an accidental stroll in the direction of Mr. Archer's house, which was but a few hundred yards distant from the village of Ripley.

Disinclined either to make fresh conquests or to meet old admirers, both contingencies being equally inconvenient at present, she followed a narrow lane skirting the backs of certain cottages, which brought her opposite the gate of Mr. Archer's garden at the exact moment when Dandy Burton, having finished his studies for the day, put a cigar into his mouth, as a light and temperate substitute for luncheon, the

Dandy—whose figure was remarkably symmetrical —being already afraid of losing his waist. Miss Draper, as she would have expressed herself, "took more than one good look at him before she played her first card;" for the hawk, though unhooded, so to speak, and flung aloft, had not yet made quite sure of her quarry, and, except as a question of wholesome practice, it would be a pity to waste much blandishment upon the wrong young gentleman. So she scanned him carefully before she pounced, approving much of what she saw.

Dandy Burton was tall, well-made, and undoubtedly good-looking, with an air, extremely becoming when people are not yet twenty, of being over his real age. His face was very nearly handsome, but there was something wanting in its expression, and a woman's eye would have preferred many a plainer countenance which carried a more marked impress of the man within.

Even Fanny was conscious of this defect at a second glance. It made her part, she reflected, all the easier to play. So gathering some violets from the hedge-side, she tied them coquettishly into a posy, and then, dropping a curtsey, shot a killing glance at the Dandy, while she observed, demurely enough—

"One of Mr. Archer's young gentlemen, I believe? I'm sure I ask your pardon, sir, if you're
not."

Dandy Burton, thus challenged, ranged up alongside.

"I am staying with Mr. Archer at present," said
he, removing the cigar from his mouth and making
a faint snatch at his round shooting-hat. "Did you
want to speak to any of us? I beg your pardon—I
mean, can I be of any service to you before Mr.
Archer goes out?"

With all the *savoir-vivre* he used to boast of in
the pupil-room, Mr. Burton was a little puzzled.
She was good-looking, she was well got-up, yet
something in his instincts told him she was not
quite a lady after all.

"It's not Mr. Archer," she answered, with a
becoming little blush and a laugh; "it's the young
gentleman as father bade me leave a message for—
father, down at Ripley Mill, you know, sir."

"Bad English. Talks of 'father' and calls me
'sir,'" thought the Dandy, his confidence returning
at once.

"All right, my dear," he answered, replacing the
cigar in his mouth, and crossing the road to her

side: "I know Ripley Mill well enough, and I know 'father,' as you call him, meaning, I suppose, my friend Mr. Draper; but I did not know he'd got such a little duck of a daughter. I wish I'd found it out, though, six months ago—I do, upon my honour!"

"Well, I'm sure!" replied Miss Fanny, in no way taken aback by the familiar tone of admiration; to which she was well-accustomed. "You gentlemen are so given to compliments, there's no believing a word you say. I should like to hear, now, what good it would have done you if you had known as I was down at the Mill six months ago."

"I should have walked over there every day, on the chance of seeing your pretty face!" answered the Dandy, rising, as he flattered himself, to the occasion.

"You wouldn't have found *me*," she laughed; "I've been in London since then. I only came home for good yesterday evening."

"Then I shall spend all my spare time at the Mill now, till I go away," retorted Burton, rolling the wet end of his cigar with his best air.

"Are you going away so soon?" she said, looking rather anxiously into his face.

"Decidedly," thought the Dandy, "this is a case
of love at first sight. It's deuced odd, too. I am
not much used to their ways, and it's just possible
she may be gammoning a fellow all the time. Never
mind! two can play at that game, so here goes."

"Not unless you'll come with me," he exclaimed
affectionately. "Since I've seen you, Miss Draper,
for I suppose you are Miss Draper, I couldn't bear
to leave you. Now, touching this message. Are
you quite sure you have brought it all this way
without spilling any of it?"

"I'm not one as isn't to be trusted," answered
the lady, meaningly, motioning him at the same
time to walk a little farther down the lane, out of
sight of Mr. Archer's top windows. "They say as
women can't keep secrets—I wish somebody would
try me. It's not in my nature to deceive. There,
what a fool I am, to go talking on to a gentleman
like you, and I never set eyes on you before."

"But you'll let me come and see you down at the
Mill?" said he; "it is but a step, you know, from
here. I could easily be there every day about this
time."

"And I should like to know what father would
say!" interposed Miss Fanny, with a sudden access

of propriety. " I ought to be back with father now, and here I am, putting off my time talking to you, and—there, I declare, I'm quite ashamed. I don't even know your name. It's Mr. Ainslie, isn't it ? "

Burton laughed.

" Why do you think it's Ainslie? "

" Because they told me as Mr. Ainslie was the only grown-up gentleman here," she answered, hazarding a supposition that could not fail to be favourably received, and flattering herself she was going on swimmingly.

The Dandy, however, did not see the advantage of being taken for his friend, and thought it right to undeceive his new flame without delay.

" My name's Burton," he said, rather conceitedly. " Ainslie's a shorter chap, with darker hair and eyes —altogether, not quite so—not quite so—— " he hesitated, for, though vain, he was not a fool.

" Not quite so much of a ladies' man, I dare say! " She finished his sentence for him with a laugh, to cover her own vexation, for she felt she had been wasting time sadly. " I don't think you're one as is ever likely to be mistook for somebody else. I must wish you good day now, sir. It's more than time I was back. I couldn't stay another minute if it was ever so."

She was a little disappointed at his ready acquiescence.

"And your message?" he asked, lighting a fresh cigar.

"It was only father's duty," she answered. "I was to tell the young gentlemen they're welcome to a day's fishing above Ripley Lock to-morrow, if they like to come, and there ought to be some sport for 'em, says father, if the wind keeps southerly."

"We'll be there!" answered the Dandy, joyfully. "And I say, how about luncheon? *You'll* bring it us, won't you, from the Mill?"

"For how many?" asked Miss Fanny; thinking, perhaps, it might not be a bad plan.

"Well, there's three of us!" answered the Dandy. "Dolly, and Ainslie, and me. Better bring enough for four, Miss Draper. It's not every day in the week I do such things. Besides, you'll sit down with us, you know, or we shan't be able to eat a morsel."

She tossed her head. "Indeed, you're very kind," she said. "Well, if you're all coming, I'll attend to it, and perhaps bring it you myself. No, sir! not

a step further. I couldn't think of walking through
the village with you. What would Mr. Archer say?
Thank you; I can take very good care of myself!"

Thus parrying the Dandy's importunities, who,
having nothing better to do, proposed a lounge
down to the Mill in her company, Miss Draper proceeded on her homeward journey, only turning round
when she had gone a few steps, to comply with his
entreaties that she would give him her lately-
gathered posy.

"You'll chuck us the violets, at least," said this
young gentleman, in a plaintive tone.

"Yes; I don't want the violets," she answered,
not very graciously, and whisking past the turn by
the baker's, was soon out of sight.

Dandy Burton was so elated with this, his last
conquest, that he did not even wait to finish his
cigar, but throwing it away, returned hastily to
the pupil-room in order to catch his companions
before they went out.

He was lucky enough to find them both still in
their studies; Gerard Ainslie struggling hard with
"unknown quantities," and Dolly puzzling over
the discovery of America, an era of history in-
separable, in his own mind, from the destruction

of the Spanish Armada. Burton had no scruple in disturbing them.

"Look there, you chaps!" said he, throwing Fanny Draper's violets on the study-table. "That's the way to do it! A fellow can't even smoke a quiet weed in these diggings, but he's pelted in again with flowers! Now I don't mind laying odds, neither of you can tell in three guesses where these came from."

"Don't bother!" answered Ainslie, looking up impatiently, and diving once more head-foremost into his algebra.

> " Some flowerets of Eden we still inherit,
> But the trail of *the Dandy* is over them all ! "

quoted Dolly, shutting up his English History with a sigh of relief. " Why they were given you by ' some village maiden who with dauntless breast ' was determined on making you a greater fool, my beloved Dandy, than nature and Archer combined can accomplish—if such a feat were, indeed, possible. They can't let him alone, ochone ! Every institution has its show-man, you know, Jerry, and the Dandy is ours ! "

Gerard did not think it worth while to answer;

and Burton, on whose good-humoured self-conceit
the arrows of chaff rained harmless, replied,
"Wouldn't you like it yourself, Dolly? Never
mind, my boy. Every chap must paddle his own
canoe. We all have different gifts, you know."

"Very true," replied Dolly. "Dress and deportment are yours; light literature, I think, is mine;
and," sinking his voice while he jerked his head
towards Ainslie, "love and logarithms are his!"

"Wake up, Jerry!" exclaimed Burton, "and
answer this slanderous accusation. Of logarithms
we acquit you at once, and surely you are not soft
enough to be in love!"

Ainslie reddened. "Well," he said, keeping down
his confusion, "I suppose a fellow may have 'a spoon'
if he likes."

"A spoon!" exclaimed Dolly. "A regular soup-
ladle! He's got all the symptoms—premonitory,
sympathetic, and confirmed.

There is even a space for the ghost of her face in this narrow
    pupil-room,
And Archer is blind, and the Dandy's a fool, and Jerry
    has met with his doom."

"What nonsense you talk!" retorted Ainslie,
angrily. "At all events, I don't pick a handful of

violets to flash them down on the study-table, and
swear they were given me by a duchess five minutes
ago. Hang it! mine should be a better swagger
than that. I'd have roses or pinks, or a bunch of
hot-house flowers, when I was about it."

> " A primrose on the river's brim,
> A yellow primrose is to him,
> And in he goes to sink or swim,"

observed Dolly. " One flower is as good as another,
if it's offered by the right party. Now I know
where Dandy got these. They were given him by
the cook. She picks them for the salad, and puts
them in with what she calls 'garnishing'—slugs,
eggshell, and bits of gravel."

" You know nothing about it, Dolly!" exclaimed
Ainslie. " This isn't a salad-day. No; it's a keepsake from Mother Markham,—milliner and *modiste*.
She's repaired Dandy's stays ever so often since he
came."

" You're wrong, both of you," said the imperturbable Dandy. " They were given me by Miss
Draper—Miss Fanny Draper, of Ripley Mill—now
then ! A young lady neither of you have ever seen ;
and a deuced pretty girl too. What's more, she
asked if my name wasn't Ainslie?"

Again Gerard blushed, and this time without cause.

"A most improbable story," remarked Dolly. "Ainslie's engaged. If she'd said Egremont, I could have believed it. This requires confirmation."

" I can prove it fast enough," answered Burton. "Old 'Grits' wants us all to go down and fish at the Upper Lock to-morrow. It won't be bad fun. I vote we go, if Nobs will stand it. He must let us out at twelve o'clock."

"You'd better ask him, Dolly," said Gerard. "Here he comes!"

While the latter spoke, Mr. Archer entered the pupil-room with a listless air, and rather a weary step. Truth to tell, he was a little tired of the ever-recurring round which in the slang of to-day is not inappropriately termed a "grind." It paid him well, as he often said to himself, or it would be unbearable. Like the treadmill, or any such penal labour, it was hard work with no visible result. One pupil after another was indeed turned out, just able to squeeze through his examination, as a chair or a table is finished off to order by a carpenter; but that result attained, the master's duty was done by his disciple, and he had no further interest in the latter's progress or subsequent career. Slow and quick, stupid and clever, all had to be brought up to exactly the same standard,—the former required more time and pains than the latter, that was the whole difference. One can scarcely conceive a more uninteresting phase of tutorship.

Archer had made an improvident marriage, and a very happy one ; had sold out of the Army in consequence, and had been glad to augment his slender income by fitting young men for the profession he had left. But his wife died early, and with her the stimulus to exertion was gone. He had no children, and few friends. Altogether it was weary work.

If the necessary amount of study could be got through in the week, a holiday was even a greater relief to tutor than pupils ; and with a stipulation to that effect, he willingly granted Dolly's request that they should all start on their fishing excursion next day at twelve o'clock.

CHAPTER VII.

A CAT'S-PAW.

OLD "GRITS," as his familiars called that very
respectable miller, Mr. Draper, liked to have his
breakfast early — really early; meaning thereby
somewhere about sunrise. This entailed getting up
in the dark on such of his household as prepared
that meal, and Miss Fanny entertained the greatest
objection to getting up in the dark. Consequently,
as they breakfasted together—for on this the miller
insisted while she stayed with him—both father and
daughter were put out from their usual habits. The
hour was too early for her, too late for him. He was
hungry and snappish, she was hurried and cross.
Whatever differences of opinion they entertained
were more freely discussed, and more stoutly upheld
at this, than at any other hour of the twenty-four.

It is a great thing to begin the day in good humour; and that woman is wise, be she mother, wife, or daughter, who brings a smiling face down to breakfast ere the toast becomes sodden and the tea cold; who, if she has disagreeable intelligence to communicate, grievances to detail, or complaints to make, puts them off till the things have been taken away, and an evil can be confronted in that spirit of good-will and good-humour which robs it of half its force. Put man, woman, or child, or even a dumb animal, wrong the first thing in the morning, and the equanimity thus lost is seldom restored till late in the afternoon. Grits and Fanny both knew this well by experience, yet they had their say out just the same.

"Now, Fan!" grunted the miller, walking heavily into their little parlour, with a cloud of yesterday's flour rising from his clothes. "Look alive, girl! Come—bustle, bustle! It's gone six o'clock."

"Why, father, how you keep on worriting!" replied a voice from an inner chamber, constrained and indistinct, as of one who is fastening her stays, with hair-pins in her mouth.

"Worriting indeed!" retorted Mr. Draper. "It's been broad daylight for more than an hour. I should like to know how a man is to get his work done, if his breakfast has to be put back till nigh dinner-time. These may be quality manners, lass; but blow me if they suits us down here at Ripley!"

"Blow your tea, father—that's what you've got to blow," replied Miss Fanny, who had now emerged from her tiring-room only half-dressed, pouring him out a cup so hot that it was transferred, to be operated on as she suggested, into the saucer. "I do believe now, if it wasn't for me coming here to stop with you at odd times, you'd get your breakfast so early as it would interfere with your supper over-night!"

The miller was busy with thick bread-and-butter. A growl was his only reply. Miss Fanny looked out of the window thoughtfully, drank a little tea, shot a doubtful glance at her papa, and hazarded the following harmless question:

"It's a dull morning, father. Do you think it will hold up—you that knows the weather so well at Ripley?"

It pleased him to be esteemed wise on such matters, and the hot tea had put him in a better humour.

"Hold up, lass?" he answered, cheerfully; "why

shouldn't it hold up? Even with a south wind, these here grey mornings doesn't often turn to rain. You may put your best bonnet on to-day, Fan, never fear!"

"Then, if that's the case, I'll get the house-work over in good time; and I think I won't be back to dinner, father," said his daughter resolutely, as anticipating objection.

But for its coating of flour the miller's face would have darkened.

"Not back to dinner, Fan! And why not? Where may you be going, lass, if I may make so bold as ask?"

She hesitated a moment, and then observed very demurely—

"I took your message up to Mr. Archer's yesterday, and the young gentlemen's coming down to fish, as you kindly invited of 'em——"

"I know—I know," said he. "Well, lass, and what then?"

"They're to be at water-side by twelve o'clock, and I'll engage they'll keep on till sun-down. Poor little chaps! They'll be wanting their dinners, and I thought I'd best step out and take 'em some."

"Poor little chaps!" repeated the miller. "Why,

one of 'em 's six feet high, and t'other 's nigh
twenty years old; and Mr. Egremont—that's him
as comes down by times for a smoke here—well,
he'll pull down as heavy a weight as I can; and
I dare say, for his years, he's nigh as sensible.
They're grown-up young gentlemen, Fan, every
man of 'em."

"They'll want their dinners all the same," answered Fan.

"And they'll want you to take 'em their dinners,
I daresay; and want must be their master!" replied
the miller. "I don't like it, Fan, I tell 'ee—I
don't like it. What call have you to go more nor a
mile up water-side after three young sparks like
them? I may be behind the times, Fan—I daresay
as I am; but it can't be right. I don't like it, I
tell 'ee, lass, and I won't have it!"

"I'm not a child, father," answered the girl in
perfect good-humour. "I should think I can take
care of myself in uglier places than Ripley Lock;
and I was going on to see the housekeeper at Oakover, whether or no. However, if you think well,
I'll send Jane with the basket; only she's wanted in
the house, let alone that she's young and giddy;
and if I was you, father, I'd sooner trust me nor her."

"I can get serving-lasses by the score," answered old Draper very gruflly, because a tear was twinkling in the corner of his eye, "but I have only one daughter. I've been a kind father to you, Fan, ever since you and me used to watch the big wheel together when you was too little to go up the mill-steps. Don't ye come a-flyin' in my face because you've growed up into a fine likely young woman— don't ye now!"

She was touched; she couldn't help it. She went round the table, and put her hand on the old man's shoulder. For the moment she was willing to be a dutiful and affectionate child.

"You *have* been a kind old daddy," she said, turning his dusty face up to kiss it; "and I wouldn't vex you for that kettleful of gold. But you won't mind my stepping across to Oakover—now, will you, father? And I'll be sure to come back and give you your tea."

She knew exactly how to manage him.

"You're a good lass, I do believe," said he, rising from the table, "and a sensible one, too; maybe, more nor I think for. Well, there'll be no harm in your taking a basket of prog, and leaving it at the Lock for them young chaps. But don't ye go

a-fishin' along of 'em, there's a good lass ! Folk *will*
talk, my dear. Why, they'll hardly let me alone
when I give Widow Bolt a lift home from market
in the cart. Now, hand us a light for the pipe, Fan.
I've said my say, so I'm off to my work; and I'll
leave you to yours."

But Mr. Draper shook his head, nevertheless,
while he walked round by the mill-sluice, smoking
thoughtfully.

" She's wilful," he muttered—" wilful ; and so
was her mother. Most on 'em 's wilful, as I see.
I'm thankful the boys is doing so well. They're
good sons to me, they are. And yet—and yet I'd
sooner both on 'em was sold up—I'd sooner see the
river run dry, and the mill stop work—I'd sooner
lose the close, and the meadow, and the house, and
the stock—than that anything should go wrong
with little Fan ! "

Little Fan in the meantime, having gained her
point, was in high good-humour. She sang merrily
over what trifling work she chose to do about the
house, abstaining from harsh words to Jane, who
whenever she had a spare moment seemed to be
peeling potatoes. She packed a basket with eatables,
and filled a bottle with wine, for the anglers. Then

she attired herself in a very becoming dress, put on a pair of well-fitting gloves, not quite new, just like a real lady's, she told herself, and crowned the whole with a killing little bonnet. Anybody meeting Miss Draper as she sauntered leisurely along the river-side with her basket in her hand would have taken her for the Rector's young wife, or the Squire's daughter at the least.

Even the anglers were something dazzled by this brilliant apparition. Burton, proud of his acquaintance made the day before, felt yet a little abashed by so fascinating an exterior. Ainslie scanned her attentively, but this, I imagine, chiefly because her bonnet reminded him of Norah's; while Dolly, who was getting very hungry, took off his hat with a polite bow, observing in a low voice, for the benefit of his companions—

> " It was the miller's daughter,
>   And she stoppeth one of three
>   On the banks of Allan-water—
>   How I wish that it was me ! "

Miss Draper's deportment in presence of three strange young gentlemen was a model of propriety and good taste. She simply vouchsafed a curtsey, to be divided amongst them; offered her father's good

wishes for their sport; and proceeded to unpack her
basket without delay. "For," said she, "I have
no time to spare. I am going a little farther up-
stream on an errand, and will call for the basket as
I come back." Nevertheless, though her eyes seemed
fastened on her occupation, she had scanned each of
them from top to toe in two minutes, and learned
the precise nature of the ground on which she was
about to manœuvre.

Burton's name she had already learnt. One glance
at Dolly Egremont's jolly face satisfied her that with
him she could have no concern. It must be the slim,
well-made lad with the dark eyes and pleasant smile,
whom she had engaged to subjugate. No disagreeable duty neither, thought Miss Fanny; so she set
about it with a will.

Leaving her basket in charge of Dolly, who
pledged himself with great earnestness for its safety,
she walked leisurely up-stream, and was pleased to
observe that the three anglers separated at once; his
two companions choosing different sides of the river
below the mill, while Gerard Ainslie followed the
upward bend of the stream, not having yet put his
rod together, nor unwound the casting-line from his
hat. He was thinking but little of his fishing, this

infatuated young man ; certainly not the least of
Miss Fanny Draper. No. The gleam on the water,
the whisper of the sedges, the swallows dipping and
wheeling at his feet, all the soft harmony of the
landscape, all the tender beauty of the early summer,—what were these but the embodiment of his
ideal ? And his ideal, he fancied, was far away
yonder, across the marshes, thinking, perhaps, at
that very moment, of him ! She was not across the
marshes, as we shall presently see, but within half
a mile of where he stood. Nevertheless, what would
love be without illusion ? And is not the illusion a
necessary condition of the love ? Look at a soap-
bubble glowing in the richest tints of all the gems
of earth and sea. Presently, behold, it bursts.
What becomes of the tints? and where, oh ! where
is the bubble ?

Gerard was roused from his dreams by the rustle
of a feminine garment, and the sudden appearance
of the miller's daughter lying in wait for him at the
very first stile he had to cross. She knew better
than to give a little half-suppressed start, as when
she met Vandeleur, or to display any of the affecta-
tions indulged in by young women of her class ; for,
wherever she picked it up, Miss Draper had acquired

considerable knowledge of masculine nature, and was well aware that while timidity and innocence are efficient weapons against the old, there is nothing like cool superiority to overawe and impose upon the young.

She took his rod out of his hand, as a matter of course, while he vaulted the stile, and observed quietly—" I saw you coming, Mr. Ainslie, and so I waited for you. I suppose as you're not much acquainted with our river; there's a pool, scarce twenty yards below the bridge, yonder, where you'll catch a basket of fish in ten minutes, if you've any luck."

She looked very pretty in the gleams of sunlight with her heightened colour, and her black hair set off by the transparency she called a bonnet. Even to a man in love she was no despicable companion for an hour's fly-fishing; and Gerard thanked her heartily, asking her, if their ways lay together, to walk on with him, and point out the place. His smile was very winning, his voice low and pleasant, his manner to women soft and deferential—such a manner as comes amiss with neither high nor low: to a duchess, fascinating, to a dairy-maid, simply irresistible. Miss Draper stole a look at him from

under her black eye-lashes, and liked her job more
and more.

"I'll come with you, and welcome," said she,
frankly. "The walk's nothing to me; I'm used to
walking. I'm a country-bred girl, you know, Mr.
Ainslie, though I've seen a deal of life since I left
the Mill."

"Then you don't live at the Mill?" said Gerard,
absently, for that unlucky bonnet had taken his
thoughts across the marshes again.

"I do when I'm at home," she answered, "but
I'm not often at home. I've got my own bread to
make, Mr. Ainslie, if I don't want to be a burden
to father. And I don't neither. I'm not like a
real lady, you know, that can sit with her hands
before her, and do nothing. But you mustn't think
the worse of me for that, must you?"

"Of course not!" he answered, as what else could
he answer? wondering the while why this handsome
black-eyed girl should thus have selected him from
his companions for her confidences.

"I shouldn't be here now," she continued, "if it
wasn't to see how father gets on. There's nothing
but father to bring me back to such a dull place as
Ripley. Yet, dull as it is, I can tell you, Mr.

Ainslie, you must mind what you're at if you don't want to be talked about!"

"I suppose you and I would be talked about now," said he, laughing, "if we could be seen."

"*I* don't mind, if you don't!" she answered, looking full in his eyes. "Well, our walk's over now, at any rate. There's the bridge, and here's the pool. I've seen my brothers stand on that stone, and pull 'em out a dozen in an hour!"

There was something of regret in her tone when she announced the termination of their walk that was sufficiently pleasant to his ear. He could not help looking gratified, and she saw it; so she added, "If you'll put your rod together, I'll sort your tackle the while. They've queer fancies, have *our* fish, all the way from here to Ripley Lock; and they won't always take the same fly you see on the water. They're feeding now—look!"

So the two sat down together on a large stone under a willow, with the stream rippling at their feet, and the hungry trout leaping like rain-drops, all across its surface—in the shadow of the opposite bank, in the pool by the water-lilies, under the middle arch of the bridge, everywhere just beyond the compass of a trout-rod and its usual length of

line. Gerard's eye began to glisten, for he was a
fisherman to the backbone. He had put his rod
together, and was running the tackle through its
top joint when his companion started and turned
pale.

" Is that thunder ? " said she. " Listen ! "

" Thunder ! " repeated the busy sportsman, contemptuously. " Pooh ! nonsense ! It's only a
carriage."

Miss Draper was really afraid of thunder, and felt
much relieved.

" Haven't you a green drake ? " she asked, hunt-
ing busily over his fly-book for that killing artifice.

He stooped low to help her, and one of the hooks
in the casting-line round his hat caught in her pretty
little bonnet. They were fairly tied together by the
ears, a position that, without being at all unpleasant,
was ridiculous in the extreme. She smiled sweetly
in the comely face so close to her own, and both
burst out laughing. At that moment a pony-carriage
was driven rapidly across the bridge immediately
over against them. Gerard's head was turned away,
but its occupants must have had a full view of the
situation, and an excellent opportunity of identify-
ing the laughers. The lady who drove it immedi-

ately lashed her ponies into a gallop, bowing her head low over her hands as if in pain.

Gerard sprang to his feet.

"Did you see that carriage, Miss Draper?" he exclaimed hurriedly. "Had it a pair of cream-coloured ponies?"

"Cream-coloured ponies!" repeated Fanny, innocently. "I believe they was. I think as it were Miss Welby, from Marston Rectory."

His violent start had broken the casting-line, and he was free. Like a deer, he sprang off in pursuit of the carriage, running at top-speed for nearly a quarter of a mile. But the cream-coloured ponies were in good condition and well-bred,—with a sore and jealous heart immediately behind them, which controlled, moreover, a serviceable driving-whip. He could never overtake them, but laid himself down panting and exhausted on the grass by the road-side, after a two-mile chase.

When Gerard went back for his rod, Miss Draper was gone; but he had no heart for any more fishing the rest of that afternoon.

CHAPTER VIII.

HOT CHESTNUTS.

ASTOUNDED at her companion's unceremonious departure, the miller's daughter stood for a while motionless, her bright face darkening into an expression of vexation, not to say disgust. Half-immersed, the neglected trout-rod lay at her feet, paying its line out slowly to the gentle action of the stream. Something in the click of the reel perhaps aroused the thriftier instincts of her nature. She stooped to extricate rod and tackle with no unpractised hand, laid them on the bank ready for his return, and then sat down again to think. Till within the last few minutes Miss Draper had been well pleased. Not averse to flirting, she would have consented, no doubt, to take in hand any of Mr. Archer's young gentlemen; but her walk with

Gerard Ainslie, though shorter, was also sweeter than she expected. The refinement of his tone, his gestures, his manner altogether, was extremely fascinating, because so unlike anything to which she was accustomed. "He's not so handsome as t'other," soliloquised Miss Draper, "for I make no count of the fat one" (thus putting Dolly ignominiously out of the race), "but his hair is as soft as a lady's, and his eyes is like velvet. He's a nice chap, that! but whatever made him start away like mad after Miss Welby and her pony-carriage? I wonder whether he'll come back again. I wonder what odds it makes to me whether he comes back or no? Well, I've no call to be at the mill till tea-time. I'll just step on and gather a few violets at Ashbank. Perhaps the young man would like a posy to take with him when he goes home!"

She recollected, almost with shame, how willingly she had given away another posy of violets to his fellow-pupil so short a time ago.

Ashbank was a narrow belt of wood separating the meadow from the high-road. She had gathered many a wild flower under its tall trees, had listened to many a rustic compliment, borne her full share of many a rustic flirtation, in its sheltering depths.

For the first time in her life she wished it otherwise; she wished she had held her head a little higher, kept her clownish admirers at a more respectful distance. Such conquests, she now felt, were anything but conducive to self-respect. She rose from her seat impatiently, and it was with a heightened colour and quick, irregular steps, that she trod the winding footpath leading to the wood.

She had never before thought the scenery about Ripley and its neighbourhood half so pretty. To-day there was a fresher verdure in the meadow, softer whispers in the woodland, a fairer promise in the quiet sky. She could not have analysed her feelings, was scarce conscious of them, far less could she have expressed their nature; yet she felt that for her, as for all of us, there are moments when

" A livelier emerald twinkles in the grass,
A purer sapphire melts into the sea;"

and this was one of them.

There is a certain fire dreaded by burnt children, and often kindled by the tiniest spark, at which it is unspeakable comfort to warm the hands, but with the glow of which people never seem satisfied till they have burnt their fingers. Like other fires, it should be poked sparingly, is easily smothered with over-much fuel, and burns, I think, fiercest in the hardest weather. Also, though a good servant, it is a bad master; carefully to be watched, lest it spread to a conflagration; scarring deep where it scorches, to leave the sufferer marked and disfigured for a life-time.

Of that fire the miller's daughter had been hitherto unconscious. She had always stood, as yet, on higher ground than those of the other sex, whatever their station, on whom she had thought it worth while to exercise her fascinations. It was capital fun then. It was all mirth, merry-making, rivalry, and gratified vanity. Was it good fun now? She had already asked herself that question, though she had scarcely spent half an hour in the society of her new acquaintance. Already she had answered, No! It was something better than fun, this—something deeper, sweeter, and far more dangerous. The first time a swimmer trusts to his newly-acquired art, he exults, no doubt, in the excitement of his situation, the development of his power; but want of confidence in himself is the sure symptom that proves to him he is out of his depth. So was it now with Fanny. She longed for a mirror in which to arrange her hair, dishevelled by the south wind. She con-

demned the bonnet she had thought so killing an
hour ago; she mistrusted her very muslin; she
thought her gloves looked soiled and her boots un-
tidy. She wondered whether he had detected free-
dom in her manner, want of education in her speech.
She had often before wished she was a lady, but it
was only that she might roll in a carriage, wear
expensive dresses, and order about a quantity of
servants. Now she felt as if she had over-rated the
value of all these things, that silks, and splendour,
and liveries were not the sole accessories of good
breeding; and yet she wanted to be a lady more
than ever. Why? Because Mr. Ainslie was a
gentleman.

Thus, wishing, and dreaming, and repining, walking fast all the while, her colour was higher and
her temper less equal than usual when she reached
the shadows of Ashbank, and climbed the stile she
had crossed so often on similar expeditions after
hazel-nuts or wild flowers in days gone by. Sur-
mounting the obstacle less carefully than she might
have done had she expected a looker-on, it cooled
neither her face nor her temper to find Mr. Vandeleur strolling quietly through the copse, smoking a
cigar with his usual air of careless good-humoured

superiority. She bounced off the foot-board, and
putting her head down, tried to pass him without
speaking, but he stretched his arms across the path,
and stopped her with a laugh.

Her eyes flashed angrily when she looked up in
his face.

"I do believe as you're the devil!" exclaimed
the girl, in a voice that seemed to denote she was in
earnest.

"I appreciate the compliment, Miss Fanny," said
he, removing the cigar from his mouth. "But I
assure you I am not, all the same. *You* are an
angel though, my dear. I did not expect you for at
least an hour, and as I hate waiting, I am grateful
for your early appearance."

"I shouldn't have come at all only I promised,"
answered Miss Fanny in a disturbed voice. "And,
there, I wish I hadn't come at all as it is! I wish
I hadn't met you in Ripley Lane! I wish I'd never
set eyes on you in my life! I wish—what's the use
of wishing?"

"What, indeed?" replied Vandeleur. "I should
have lost a very agreeable little acquaintance; you,
a tolerably useful friend. Something has gone
wrong, Miss Fanny, I'm afraid. You seem put

out, and it's very becoming, I give you my honour.
Sit down, and tell us all about it."

"I'll not sit down, Mr. Vandeleur," protested
the miller's daughter, glancing anxiously towards
the river she had left. "But I'll walk as far as the
end of the wood with you. I suppose as you've got
something particular to say, since you've kept your
appointment so correct."

"Quite right," he answered. "Something very
particular, and it won't bear delay neither. There's
no time to be lost. I want to know how you're
getting on?"

Miss Draper controlled herself with an effort, and
spoke in a hard clear voice.

"I did what you told me. I went to Mr. Archer's
yesterday, and made acquaintance with the young
gentleman to-day."

"With Gerard Ainslie?" he asked.

She nodded, and her colour rose.

"What do you think of him?" continued Vandeleur, smiling.

"I don't think about him at all," she flashed out.
"Oh, Mr. Vandeleur, it's a shame; it's a shame!
And it can't be done neither! I do believe as he's
one to love the very ground a girl walks on!"

The smile deepened on his face. "Likely enough," said he quietly, "but that won't last long now he has seen *you*."

She looked a little better pleased. "Such nonsense!" she exclaimed. "What can I do?"

"This is what you can do," replied Vandeleur, never lifting his eyes higher than her boots, "and nobody else about here, or I should not have asked you. You can detach the boy from his foolish fancy as easily as I can break off this convolvulus. Look here. If it won't unwind, it must be torn asunder. If you can't work with fair means, you must use foul."

While he spoke he tore the growing creepers savagely with his fingers, laughing more than the occasion seemed to warrant. Though she could not see how his eyes gleamed, she wondered at this exuberance of mirth. Strangely enough, it seemed to sober and subdue her.

"Tell me what to do, sir," said she quietly, with a paler cheek. "You've been a good friend to me, and I'm not an ungrateful girl, Mr. Vandeleur, indeed."

"You must attach young Ainslie to yourself," he replied in the most matter-of-course tone. "It ought

not to be a difficult job, and I shouldn't fancy it can
be an unpleasant one. Tell the truth now, Miss
Fan, wouldn't you like to have the silly boy over
head and ears in love with you?"

She turned her face away, and made no answer.
Looking under her bonnet, he saw that she was
crying.

"Do you think I have no self-respect?" she
asked, in a broken voice.

"I know *I* haven't," he answered, "but that's no
rule for you. Look ye here, Miss Fanny, business
is business. I shouldn't have brought you here
without something to say. When you've done crying, perhaps you'll be ready to hear it."

"I'm ready now," she replied, with a steady look
in his face that he did not endure for half-a-second.

"I gave you a month when we met the other
evening, but I've altered my mind since then. If
you'll halve the time, I'll double the money. There,
you won't meet so fair an offer as that every day in a
market. What say you, Miss Fan? Are you game?"

She was walking with her hands clasped, and
twined her fingers together as if in some deep
mental conflict, but showed no other sign of distress.

"I don't like it," she said quietly, but in clear

forcible tones; " I don't like it. I could do it better
by either of the others. At least, I mean they
seem as though they wouldn't be quite so much in
earnest. And it looks such a cruel job, too, if so be
as the young lady likes him—and like him she
must, I'm sure. Who is the young lady, Mr.
Vandeleur? You promised as you'd tell me to-
day."

It was true enough. Curiosity is a strong stimu-
lant, and he had reserved this part of the scheme
to ensure Miss Draper's punctuality in keeping her
appointment.

"The young lady," replied Vandeleur. "I
thought you might have guessed. Miss Welby, of
Marston."

"Has Miss Welby got a sweetheart?" exclaimed
the other in an accent of mingled jealousy, exultation, and pique. "Well, you do surprise me. And
him! Why didn't you tell me before?"

Why, indeed? He found her much more manage-
able now. She listened to his instructions with the
utmost deference. She even added little feminine
improvements of her own. She would do her very
best, she said, and that as quickly as might be, to
further all his schemes. And she meant it too. She

was in earnest now. She understood it all. She knew why he had broken away from her so rudely, and started after the pony-carriage like a madman. It was Miss Welby, was it? And he was courting her, was he? Then Fanny Draper learned for the first time why the afternoon had been so different from the morning. She felt now that she herself loved Gerard Ainslie recklessly, as she had never loved before. And it was to be a struggle, a match, a deadly rivalry between herself and this young lady, who had all the odds in her favour, of station, manners, dress, accomplishments, every advantage over herself except a fierce, strong will, and a reckless, undisciplined heart.

When Vandeleur emerged alone from Ashbank on his way home he had no reason to be dissatisfied with the ardour of his partisan. He was not easily astonished, as he used often to declare, but on the present occasion he shook his head wisely more than once, and exclaimed in an audible voice—

"Well, I always thought Miss Fan wicked enough for anything, but I'd no idea even she could have so much devil in her as that!"

CHAPTER IX.

A PASSAGE OF ARMS.

OLD " GRITS " was seldom wrong about the weather. The wind remained southerly, and yet the rain held off. The day after the fishing party was bright and calm. Nevertheless, it smiled on two very unhappy people within a circle of three miles. The least to be pitied of this unlucky pair was Ainslie, inasmuch as his was an expected grievance, and in no way took him unawares.

When Mr. Archer granted their release the day before, it was on the express stipulation that the succeeding afternoon as well as morning should be devoted to study by his pupils, and Gerard knew that it would be impossible for him to cross the marshes for the shortest glimpse of his ladye-love till another twenty-four hours had elapsed. He could have borne his imprisonment more patiently had he not been

so disappointed in his chase after the pony-carriage,
had he not also felt some faint, shadowy misgivings
that its driver might have disapproved of the position in which she saw him placed.

It was bad enough to miss an unexpected chance
of seeing Norah ; but to think that she could believe
him capable of familiarity with such an individual
as Miss Draper, and not to be able to justify himself, because, forsooth, he was deficient in modern
history, was simply maddening. What was the
Seven Years' War, with all its alternations, to the
contest raging in his own breast? How could he
take the slightest interest in Frederic the Great,
and Ziethen, and Seidlitz, and the rest of the Prus-
sian generals, while Norah was within a league,
and yet out of reach? "What must she think of
him?" he wondered; "and what was she about?"

If Miss Welby had been asked what she was about,
she would have declared she was gathering flowers
for the house. Anybody else would have said she
was roaming here and there in an aimless, restless
manner, with a pair of scissors and a basket. Anybody else might have wondered why she could settle
to no occupation, remain in no one place for more
than five minutes at a time—why her cheek was

pale and her eyes looked sleepless; above all, why about her lips was set that scornful smile which, like a hard frost breaking up in rain, seldom softens but with a flood of tears.

Norah knew the reason—very bitter and very painful it was. We, who have gone through the usual training of life, and come out of it more or less hardened into the cynicism we call good sense, or the indolence we dignify as resignation, can scarcely appreciate the punishment inflicted by these imaginary distresses on the young. Jealousy is hard to bear even for us, encouraged by example, cased in selfishness, and fortified by a hundred worldly aphorisms. We shrug our shoulders, we even force a laugh; we talk of human weakness, male vanity or female fickleness, as the case may be; we summon pride to our aid and intrench ourselves in an assumed humility; or we plead our philosophy, which means we do not care very much for anything but our dinners. Perhaps, after all, our feelings *are* blunted. Perhaps—shame on us!—we experience the slightest possible relief from thraldom, the faintest ray of satisfaction in reflecting that we, too, have our right to change; that for us, at no distant period, will open the fresh excitement of a fresh pursuit.

But with a young girl suffering from disappointment in her first affections there are no such counterirritants as these. She steps at once out of her fairyland into a cold, bleak, hopeless world. It is not that her happiness is gone, her feelings outraged, her vanity humbled to the dust—but her trust is broken. Hitherto she has believed in good ; now she says bitterly there is no good on the face of the earth. She has made for herself an image, which she has draped like a god, and, behold ! the image is an illusion, after all—not even a stock or a stone, but a mist, a vapour, a phantom that has passed away and left a blank which all creation seems unable to fill up. It is hard to lose the love itself, but the cruel suffering is, that the love has wound itself round every trifle of her daily life. Yesterday the petty annoyance could not vex her ; yesterday the homely pleasure, steeped in that hidden consciousness, became a perfect joy. And to-day it is all over ! To-day there is a mockery in the sunbeam, a wail of hopeless sorrow in the breeze. Those gaudy flowers do but dazzle her with their unmeaning glare, and the scent of the standard-roses would go near to break her heart, but that she feels she has neither hope nor heart left.

Norah Welby had been at least half-an-hour in the garden, and one sprig of geranium constituted the whole spoils of her basket. It was a comfort to be told by a servant that a young woman was waiting to speak with her. In her first keen pangs she was disposed, like some wounded animal, to bound restlessly from place to place, to seek relief in change of scene or attitude. They had not yet subsided into the dull, dead ache that prompts the sufferer to hide away in a corner and lie there, unnoticed and motionless in the very exhaustion of pain.

Even a London footman is not generally quick-sighted, and Mr. Welby's was a country-servant all over. Nevertheless, Thomas roused himself from his reflections, whatever they might be, and noticed that his young mistress looked "uncommon queer," as he expressed it, when he announced her visitor. She did not seem to understand till he had spoken twice, and then put her hand wearily to her forehead, while she repeated, vaguely—

"A young woman waiting, Thomas? Did she give any name?"

"It's the young woman from the Mill," answered Thomas, who would have scorned to usher a person of Miss Draper's rank into his young mistress's pre-

sence with any of the forms he considered proper to
visitors of a higher standing, and who simply nodded
his head in the direction indicated for the benefit of
the new arrival, observing without further ceremony—

"Miss Welby's in the garden. Come, look sharp!
That's the road."

And now indeed Norah's whole countenance and
deportment altered strangely from what it had been
a few minutes ago. Her proud little head went
up like the crest of a knight who hears the trumpet
pealing for the onset. There even came a colour
into her fair, smooth cheek, before so pale and wan.
Her deep eyes flashed and glowed through the long,
dark lashes, and her sweet lips closed firm and resolute over the small, white, even teeth. Women
have a strange power of subduing their emotions
which has been denied to the stronger and less
impressionable sex; also, when the attack has commenced, and it is time to begin fighting in good
earnest, they get their armour on and betake them
to their skill of fence with a rapidity that to our
slower perceptions seems as unnatural as it is
alarming.

The most practised duellist that ever stood on

guard might have taken a lesson from the attitude of cool, vigilant, uncompromising defiance with which Norah received her visitor.

The latter, too, was prepared for battle. Hers, however, was an aggressive mode of warfare which requires far less skill, courage, or tactics, than to remain on the defensive; and, never lacking in confidence, she had to-day braced all her energies for the encounter. Nothing could be simpler than her appearance, more respectful than her manner, more demure than her curtsey, as she accosted Miss Welby with her eyes cast down to a dazzling bed of scarlet geraniums at her feet.

The two girls formed no bad specimens of their respective classes of beauty, while thus confronting each other—Norah's chiselled features, graceful head, and high bearing, contrasting so fairly with the comely face and bright physical charms of the miller's daughter.

"It's about the time of our Ripley children's school-feast, Miss Welby," said the latter; "I made so bold as to step up and ask whether you would arrange about the tea as usual."

Norah looked very pale, but there was a ring like steel in her voice while she replied—

"I expected you, Fanny. I knew you had come home, for I saw you yesterday."

Fanny assumed an admirable air of unconsciousness.

"Really, miss," said she. "Well, now, I was up water-side in the afternoon, and I did make sure it was your carriage as passed over Ripley Bridge."

It seemed not much of an opening; such as it was, however, Miss Welby took advantage of it. Still very grave and pale, she continued in a low distinct voice—

"I have no right to interfere, of course, but still, Fanny, I am sure you will take what I say in good part. Do you think now that your father would approve of your attending Mr. Archer's young gentlemen in their fishing excursions up the river?"

Fanny bowed her head, and managed with great skill to execute a blush.

"Indeed, miss," she faltered, "it was only one young gentleman, and him the youngest of them as goes to school with Mr. Archer."

"I am quite aware it was Mr. Ainslie, for I am acquainted with him," pursued Norah bravely enough, but, do what she would, there was a quiver of pain in her voice when she uttered his name, and for a moment Miss Draper felt a sting of compunction worse than all the jealousy she had experienced during her interview with Vandeleur the previous afternoon.

"I have no doubt, indeed I know, he is a perfectly gentleman-like person," continued the young lady, as if she was repeating a lesson; " still, Fanny, I put it to your own good sense whether it would not have been wiser to remain at the Mill with your father."

" Perhaps you're right, miss," replied the other, acting her part of innocent simplicity with considerable success; "and I'm sure I didn't mean no harm—nor him neither, I dare say. But he's such a nice young gentleman. So quiet and careful-like. And he begged and prayed of me so hard to show him the way up-stream, that indeed, miss, I had not the heart to deny him."

" Do you mean he asked you to go?" exclaimed Norah, and the next moment wished she had bitten her tongue off before it framed a question to which she longed yet dreaded so to hear the answer.

" Well, miss," replied Fanny, candidly, " I suppose a young woman ought not to believe all that's

told her by a real gentleman like Mr. Ainslie;
and yet he seems so good and kind and affable, I
can't think as he'd want to go and deceive a poor
girl like me."

Norah felt her heart sink, and a shadow, such as
she thought must be like the shadow of death, passed
over her eyes; but not for an instant did her
courage fail, nor her self-command desert her at
her need.

"It is no question of Mr. Ainslie," said she with
an unmoved face, "nor indeed of anybody in particular. I have said my say, Fanny, and I am sure
you will not be offended, so we will drop the subject,
if you please. And now, what can I do for you
about the school-feast?"

But Fanny cared very little for the school-feast, or
indeed for anything in the world but the task she
had on hand, and its probable results, as they
affected a new wild foolish hope that had lately risen
in her heart. With a persistence almost offensive,
she tried again and again to lead the conversation
back to Gerard Ainslie, but again and again she
was baffled by the quiet resolution of her companion.
She learned indeed that Miss Welby was somewhat
doubtful as to whether she should be present at

the tea-making in person, but beyond this gathered
nothing more definite as to that young lady's feelings and intentions than the usual directions about
the prizes, the usual promise of assistance to the
funds.

For a quarter of an hour or so, Norah, stretched
on the rack, bore her part in conversation on indifferent subjects in an indifferent tone, with a stoicism
essentially feminine, and at the expiration of that
period Fanny Draper departed, sufficiently well
pleased with her morning's work. She had altered
her opinion now, as most of us do alter our opinions
in favour of what we wish, and dismissed all compunction from her heart in meddling with an attachment that on one side at least seemed to have taken
no deep root. "She don't care for him, not really,"
soliloquised Miss Fanny, as the wicket-gate of the
Parsonage clicked behind her, and she turned her
steps homeward. "I needn't have gone to worrit
and fret so about it after all. It's strange too—
such a nice young gentleman, with them eyes and
hair. But she don't care for him, nobody needs
to tell me that—no more nor a stone!"

How little she knew! How little we know each
other! How impossible for one of Fanny Draper's

wilful, impulsive disposition to appreciate the haughty
reticence, the habitual self-restraint, above all, the
capability for silent suffering of that higher nature!
She thought Norah Welby did not care for Gerard
Ainslie, and she judged as nine out of ten do judge
of their fellows, by an outward show of indifference,
born of self-scorn, and by a specious composure,
partly mere trick of manner, partly resulting from
inherent pride of birth.

Norah watched the departure of her visitor without moving a muscle. Like one in a dream, she
marked the steps retiring on the gravel, the click of
the wicket-gate. Like one in a dream too, she
walked twice round the garden, pale, erect, and to
all appearance tranquil, save that now and then
putting her hand to her throat, she gasped as if for
breath. Then she went slowly into the house, and
sought her own room, where she locked the door,
and, sure that none could overlook her, flung herself down on her knees by the bedside, and wept
the first bitter, scalding, cruel tears of her young
life. Pride, scorn, pique, propriety, maidenly re-
serve, these were for the outer world, but here—
she had lost him! lost him! lost him! and the
agony was more than she could bear.

CHAPTER X.

AN APPOINTMENT.

THE post arrived at Mr. Archer's in the middle
of breakfast, and formed a welcome interruption to
the stagnation which was apt to settle on that repast.
It is not easy for a tutor to make ·conversation, day
after day, for three young gentlemen over whom he
is placed in authority, and who are therefore little
disposed to assist him in his efforts to set them at
ease. Mr. Archer could not forget that, under all
their assumed respect, he was still "Nobs" directly
his back was turned; and a man's spirit must
indeed be vigorous to flow unchecked by a consciousness that all he says and does will afford
material for subsequent ridicule and caricature.
Also, there are but few subjects in common between

three wild, hopeful boys, not yet launched in the
world, and a grave, disappointed, middle-aged man,
who has borne his share of action and of suffering,
has thought out half the illusions of life, and lived
out all its romance. If he talks gravely he bores,
if playfully he puzzles, if cynically he demoralises
them. To sink the tutor is subversive of discipline ;
to preserve that character, ruinous to good-fellow-
ship ; so long and weary silences were prone to
settle over Mr. Archer's breakfast-table, relieved
only by crunching of dry toast, applications for
more tea, and a hearty consumption of broiled bacon
and household bread. Of the three pupils, Dolly
Egremont suffered these pauses with the most impatience, betraying his feelings by restless contor-
tions on his chair, hideous grimaces veiled by the
tea-urn from Mr. Archer's eye, and a continual looking for the postman (whose arrival could be seen
from the dining-room windows), unspeakably suggestive of a cheerless frame of mind described by
himself as suppressed bore.

Glancing for the hundredth time down the laurel-
walk to the green gate, he pushed his plate away
with a prolonged yawn, nudged Gerard, who sat
beside him, with an energy that sent half that young

gentleman's tea into his breast-pocket, and burst
forth as usual in misquoted verse—

> " She said the day is dreary,
> He cometh not, she said ;
> None of us seem very cheery,
> And I wish I was in bed !

Do you know, sir, I think this 'weak and weary
post, bare-headed, sweating, knocking at the taverns,'
must have got drunk already, and is not coming
here at all."

Mr. Archer could not help smiling.

" How you remember things that are not of the
slightest use, Egremont," he observed. " May I ask
if you expect any letters of unusual importance this
morning ? "

" It's not that, sir," answered Dolly. " But a
Government functionary, particularly a postman, has
no right to be absent from his post. Mine is essentially a genius of method. I cannot bear anything
like irregularity."

" I am very glad to hear it," replied Mr. Archer
drily. " I should not have thought it, I confess."

" It's been my character from childhood," answered
Dolly, gravely ; " though I must allow both Jerry
here, and the Dandy, give me many an anxious

moment on that score.   Not to mention the postman—

I hold that man the worst of public foes
Who—look out, here he comes ! yes, there he goes ! "

Everybody laughed, for Dolly was a privileged
buffoon, and a servant entering at the moment
with the bag, there was a general anxiety evinced
while Mr. Archer unlocked it and distributed the
contents.   Three for himself, none for Dolly, two for
Burton, and one for Gerard Ainslie.

The latter started and blushed up to his temples
with surprise and pleasure.   It was the first
" Official " he had ever received, and its envelope,
fresh from the Horse Guards, was stamped with the
important words " *On Her Majesty's Service.*"

He tore it open.   It contained a sufficiently dry
communication, informing him that he would shortly
be gazetted to an ensigncy in an infantry regiment,
and directing him to acknowledge its receipt to an
" obedient servant" whose name he was quite unable
to decipher.

He pushed the open letter across the table to
Mr. Archer, who, having just received some information of the same nature, expressed no surprise, only
observing—

"We shall be sorry to lose you, Ainslie; it is sooner than I expected. Make yourself easy about your examinations. I think you are sure to pass."

He rose from the table, and the others rushed off to the pupil-room, overwhelming their companion with questions, congratulations, and chaff.

"When must you go, Jerry?" "Are you to join directly, or will they give you leave?" "Don't you funk being spun?" "Is it a good regiment? How jolly to dine at mess every day!" "I shouldn't like to be a 'Grabby' though" (this from the Dandy); "and, after all, I'd rather be a private in the cavalry than an officer in a regiment of *feet!*"

It was obvious that Granville Burton's range of experience had never included stable-duty, and that he was talking of what he knew nothing about.

Gerard Ainslie felt the *esprit de corps* already rising strong within him.

"Don't you jaw, Dandy," he replied indignantly. "You're not in the service at all yet; and I've always heard mine is an excellent regiment."

"How do you know?" laughed Dolly. "You've scarcely been in it a quarter of an hour. Never mind, Jerry, we shall be sorry to lose you. This old pupil-room will be uncommon slow with nobody but

me and Dandy to keep the game alive. The Dandy
has not an idea beyond tobacco—

> Yet it shall be—I shall lower to his level day by day,
> All that's fine within me growing coarse by smoking pipes
>   of clay."

"Pipes, indeed!" exclaimed Burton literally.
"I don't believe any fellow in the army smokes
better weeds than mine. You told me yourself,
Dolly, yesterday, under the willows, that you never
enjoyed a cigar so much as the one I gave you——"

> "Oh! it was sweet, my Granville, to catch the landward
>   breeze,
> A-swing with good tobacco, by the mill beneath the trees,
> While I spooned the miller's daughter, and we listened to
>   the roar
> Of the wheel that broke the water—and we voted you a
>   bore!"

replied the incorrigible Dolly. "Yes, you have a
certain glimmering of intellect as regards the Vir-
ginian plant, but I shall miss old Jerry awfully, just
the same. So will you, so will 'Nobs,' so will Fanny
Draper. Don't blush, old man. She looked very
sweet at you the day before yesterday ; and though
the Dandy here had thrown his whole mind into his
collars, he never made a race of it from the time she

caught sight of you till the finish. Look here! We'll all go down together, and you shall wish her good-bye, and I'll have an improving conversation and a drop of mild ale with Grits—

> In yonder chair I see him sit,
> Three fingers round the old silver cup;
> I see his grey eyes twinkle yet
> At his own jest. He drinks it up.

A devilish bad jest, too! I say, can't one of you fellows quote something now? I've been making all the running, and I'm blown at last."

"It's about time you were!" observed Burton, who had some difficulty in keeping pace with his voluble companion. "You get these odds and ends of rhyme mixed up in your head, and when you go in for examination, the only thing you'll pass for will be a lunatic asylum!"

"Not half a bad club neither!" responded Dolly. "I saw a lot of mad fellows play a cricket match once—Incurable Ward against Convalescents. The Incurables had it hollow. Beat 'em in one innings. I never knew a chap so pleased as the mad doctor. Long-stop was very like 'Nobs;' and they all behaved better at luncheon than either of you fellows do. Jerry, my boy, you'll come and see us before you join. I say, come in uniform, if you can."

The propriety of following out this original suggestion might have been canvassed at great length, but for the apparition of Mr. Archer's head at the pupil-room door, summoning Ainslie to a private interview in his *sanctum*.

"You will have to start at once," observed the tutor, looking keenly at his pupil, and wondering why the natural exultation of a youth who has received his first commission should be veiled by a shadow of something like regret. "I have a letter from your great-uncle, desiring you should proceed to London, to-night, if possible. It is sharp practice, Ainslie, but you are going to be a soldier, and must accustom yourself to march on short notice. I recollect in India,—well, that's nothing to do with it. Can you be ready for the evening train?"

"The evening train!" repeated the lad; and again a pre-occupation of manner struck Mr. Archer as unusual. "Oh, yes, sir!" he said, after a pause, and added, brightening up, "I should like to come and see you again, sir, when I've passed, and wish you good-bye."

Mr. Archer was not an impressionable person, but

he was touched; neither was he demonstrative, still he grasped his pupil's hand with unusual cordiality.

"Tell the servants to pack your things," said he, " and come to me again at six o'clock for what money you want. In the meantime, if you have any farewells to make, you had better set about them. I have nothing further to detain you on my own account."

Any farewells to make! Of course he had. One farewell that rather than forego he would have forfeited a thousand commissions with a field-marshal's baton attached to each. He thought his tutor spoke meaningly, but this on reflection, he argued, must have been fancy. How should anybody have discovered his love for Norah Welby? Had he not treasured it up in his own heart, making no confidants, and breathing it only to the water-lilies on the marshes? Within ten minutes he was speeding across those well-known flats on a fleeter foot than usual, now that he had news of such importance to communicate at Marston Rectory. The exercise, the sunshine, the balmy summer air soon raised his spirits to their accustomed pitch. Many a dream had he indulged in during those oft-repeated walks to and from the presence of his ladye-love,

but the visions had never been so bright, so life-
like, and so hopeful as to-day!

He was no longer the mere schoolboy running
over during play-hours to worship in hopeless adora-
tion at the feet of a superior being. He was a
soldier, offering a future, worthy of her acceptance,
to the woman he loved; he was a knight, ready
to carry her colours exultingly to death; he was a
man who need not be ashamed of offering a man's
devotion and a man's truth to her who should hereafter become his wife. Yes; he travelled as far as
that before he had walked a quarter of a mile. To
be sure there was an immense deal to be got through
in the way of heroism and adventure indispensable
to the working out of his plans in a becoming
manner, worthy of her and of him. One scene on
which he particularly dwelt, represented a night-
attack and a storming-party, of which, of course, he
was destined to be the leader. He could see the
rockets shooting up across the midnight sky; could
hear the whispers of the men, in their great-coats,
with their white haversacks slung, mustered ready
and willing, under cover of the trenches. He was
forming them with many a good-humoured jest and
rough word of encouragement, ere he put himself

at their head ; and now, with the thunder of field-
pieces, and the rattle of small-arms, and groans and
cheers, and shouts and curses ringing in his ears,
he was over the parapet, the place was carried, the
enemy retiring, and a decorated colonel, struck down
by his own sword, lay before him, prostrate and
bleeding to the death ! A *tableau*, bright and vivid,
if not quite so natural as reality. And all this, in
order that, contrary to the usages of polite warfare,
he might strip the said colonel of his decorations,
and bring them home to lay at Miss Welby's feet !
It was characteristic, too, that he never thought of
the poor slain officer, nor the woman that may have
loved *him*.

Altogether, by the time Gerard reached the wicket-
gate in the Parsonage-wall, his own mind was made
up, that ere a few minutes elapsed he would be
solemnly affianced to Norah, and that their union
was a mere question of time. Nothing to speak of !
Say half-a-dozen campaigns, perhaps, with general
actions, wounds, Victoria Crosses, promotions, and
so on, to correspond.

Why did his heart fail him more than usual
when he lifted the latch ? Why did it sink down
to his very boots when he observed no chair, no

book, no rickety table, no work-basket, and no white muslin on the deserted lawn ?

It leaped into his mouth again though, when he saw the drawing-room windows shut, and the blinds down. Even its outside has a wonderful faculty of expressing that a house is untenanted. And long before his feeble summons at the door-bell produced the cook, with her gown unhooked and her apron fastened round her waist, Gerard felt that his walk had been in vain.

" Is Miss Welby at home ? " asked he, knowing perfectly well she was not, and giving himself up blindly to despair.

" Not at home, sir," answered the cook, proffering for the expected card a finger and thumb discreetly covered by the corner of her apron. She knew Gerard by sight, and was slightly interested in him, as " Mr. Archer's gent. what come after our young lady." She was sorry to see him look so white, and thought his voice strangely husky when he demanded, as a forlorn hope, if he could see Mr. Welby ?

" Not here, sir ; the family be gone to London," she answered, resolutely ; but added, being merciful in her strength, " They'll not be away for long, sir.

Miss Welby said as they was sure to be back in six weeks."

Six weeks! He literally gasped for breath. The woman was about to offer him a glass of water, but he found his voice at last, and muttered, more to himself than the servant, "Surely she would write to me! I wonder if I shall get a letter?"

"It's Mr. Ainslie, isn't it?" said the cook, who knew perfectly well it was. "I *do* think, sir, as there's a letter for *you* in the post-bag. I'll step in and fetch it."

So she "stepped in and fetched it." She was a kind-hearted woman. Long ago she had lovers of her own. Perhaps, even now, she had not quite given up the idea. She was not angry, though many women would have been, that Gerard forgot to thank her—seizing the precious despatch, and carrying it off to devour it by himself, without a word: on the contrary, returning to her scrubbing and her dish-scouring, she only observed, "Poor young chap!" comparing him, though disparagingly, with a former swain of her own, who was in the pork-butchering line, had a shock head of red hair, and weighed fourteen stone.

Out of sight and hearing, Gerard opened his letter

with a beating heart. Its contents afforded but cold comfort to one who had been lately indulging in visions such as his. It was dated late the night before, and ran thus :—

"DEAR MR. AINSLIE,—In case you should call on us to-morrow, papa desires me to say that we shall be on our way to London. We are going to pay Uncle Edward a visit, and it is very uncertain when we return.

"I think I caught a glimpse of you fishing at Ripley Bridge yesterday, and hope you had good sport.

"Yours sincerely,

"L. WELBY."

It was hard to bear. Though he had now a cha-racter to support as an officer and a gentleman, I shouldn't wonder if the tears came thick and fast into his eyes while he folded it up. So cold, so dis-tant, so unfeeling! And that last sentence seemed the cruellest stroke of all. Poor boy! A little more experience would have shown him how that last sentence explained the whole—would have taught him to gather from it the brightest auguries of success. Unless offended, she would never have written in so abrupt a strain; and why should she be offended, unless she cared for him? It was like a woman, not to resist inflicting that last home-thrust; yet to a practised adversary it would have exposed her weakness, and opened up her whole guard. But Gerard was no practised adversary, and he carried a very sore heart back with him across the marshes. The only consolation he could gather was that Miss Welby had gone to London, and he would find her there. In this also he betrayed the simplicity of youth. He had yet to discover that London is a very large place for a search after the person you are most desirous to see, and that, when found, the person is likely to be less interested in you there than in any other locality on the face of the earth.

CHAPTER XI.

NEITHER the threatened six weeks, nor even five of
them, had elapsed before Mr. Welby and his daughter
returned to their pretty home. She had never felt
so glad to get back in her life. Ainslie's stay in
London had been so short as to preclude the possi-
bility of his seeking Norah with any chance of success, and a combination of feelings, amongst which
predominated no slight apprehension that her father
might open the letter, prevented him from trusting
one to be forwarded to her young mistress by his
friend the cook. So Miss Welby returned to Marston
with a firm conviction that Gerard was still at Mr.
Archer's, and would cross the marshes to visit her,
fond and submissive as usual. She had forgiven
him in her own heart long ago. It hurt it too much

to bear ill-will against its lord. The first day she
was in London she found a hundred excuses for his
fancied disloyalty; the second, shed some bitter
tears over her own cold, cruel letter; by the end
of the week had persuaded herself she was quite in
the wrong, liked him better than ever, and was
dying to get home again and tell him so. She
never doubted the game was in her own hands; and
although when the time for return drew near—acce-
lerated a whole week at her request—she anticipated
the pleasure of punishing him just a little for rendering her so unhappy, it was with a steadfast purpose
to make amends thereafter by such considerate kindness as should rivet his fetters faster than before.

She had said they were to be away six weeks;
therefore, she told herself there could be no chance
of his coming over for awhile, until he had learnt
by accident they had returned. Nevertheless, on
the very first day, she established herself, with chair,
table, and work-basket, on the lawn under the lime-
tree; and was very much disappointed when tea-
time came, and he had not arrived.

Next day it rained heavily, and this she esteemed
fortunate, because, as she argued somewhat incon-
sequently, it would have prevented his coming at

any rate, and would afford another twenty-four hours
for the usual tide of country gossip to carry him the
news of her return. The following morning she
was sure of him, and her face, when she came down
to breakfast, looked as bright and pure as the summer sky itself.

It was Norah's custom to hold a daily interview
with the cook at eleven o'clock, avowedly for the
purpose of ordering dinner; that is to say, this domestic wrote down a certain *programme* on a slate,
of which, if she wished the repast to be well dressed,
it was good policy in her young lady to approve.
On these occasions the whole economy of the household came under discussion, and those arrangements
were made on which depended the excellence of the
provender, the tidiness of the rooms, the softness of
the beds, and the orderly conduct of the servants.
The third morning, then, after her arrival, the cook,
an inveterate gossip, having exhausted such congenial subjects as soap, candles, stock, dripping, and
table-linen, bethought herself of yet one more chance
to prolong their interview.

" The letters had all come to hand safe," she hoped,
"according to the directions Miss Welby left for
forwarding of them correct."

Miss Welby frankly admitted they arrived in due course.

The cook had been "careful to post them herself regular, so as there could be no mistake. All but one. She'd forgotten to mention it, and that was the very day as Miss Welby left."

Norah's heart leaped with a wild hope. Could it be possible that cruel, odious, vile production had never reached him after all?

The cook proceeded gravely to excuse herself.

"She had seen the address—it was the only letter in the box; the young gentleman come over himself that very morning, while she (the cook) was cleaning up. He seemed anxious, poor young gentleman! and looked dreadful ill, so she made bold to give it him then and there. She hoped as she done right."

Norah's cheek turned pale. He looked ill—poor, poor fellow! And he was anxious. Of course he was. No doubt he had hurried over to explain all, and had found her gone, leaving that cruel letter (how she hated it now!) to cut him to the heart. She had been rash, passionate, unkind, unjust! She had lowered both herself and him. Never mind. He would be here to-day, in an hour at the latest; and she would beg pardon, humbly, fondly, promising never to mistrust nor to vex him again. No; there were no more orders. The cook had done quite right about the letters, and they would dine at half-past seven as usual.

It was a relief to be left alone again with her own thoughts. It was a happiness to look at the lengthening shadows creeping inch by inch across the lawn, and expect him every moment now, as luncheon came and went, and the afternoon passed away. But the shadows overspread the whole lawn, the dew began to fall, the dressing-bell rang, and still no Gerard Ainslie.

Mr. Welby attributed his daughter's low spirits during dinner to reaction after the excitement of a London life. He had felt it himself many years ago, and shuddered with the remembrance even now. At dessert a bright thought struck him, and he looked up.

"It's the archery meeting to-morrow at Oakover. Isn't it, Norah? My dear, hadn't you better go?"

"I think I shall," answered Miss Welby, who fully intended it. "Perhaps Lady Baker will take me. If she can't, I must fall back on the Browns."

"My dear, I will take you myself," replied her father stoutly, while he filled his glass.

She looked pleased.

"Oh, papa, how nice! But, dear, you'll be so dreadfully bored. There's a cold dinner, you know. And the thing lasts all day, and dancing very likely at night. However, we can come away before that."

"You're an unselfish girl, Norah," said her father, "as you always were. I tell you I'll go, and I'll stay and see it out if they dance till dawn. You shall drive me there with the ponies, and they can come back and bring the brougham for us at night. No, you needn't thank me, my dear. I'm not so good as you think. I want to have a few hours in Vandeleur's library, for I'm by no means satisfied with the 'Sea-breeze Chorus' in any of my editions here. It seems clear one word at least must be wrong. The whole spirit of the 'Medea,' the 'Hecuba,' and, indeed, every play of Euripides—But I won't inflict a Greek particle—no, nor a particle of Greek—on you, my dear. Ring the bell, and let's have some tea."

So Norah went to bed, after another day of disappointment, buoyed up once more by hope,—Gerard was sure to be at the archery meeting. Mr. Archer's young gentlemen always made a point of attending these gatherings; and Dolly Egremont had, on one

occasion, even taken a prize. " Yes," thought Miss
Welby, " to-morrow, at last, I am sure to meet him.
Perhaps he is offended. Perhaps he won't speak to
me. Never mind! He'll see I'm sorry at any rate,
and he'll know that I haven't left off caring for him.
Yes, I'll put on that lilac he thought so pretty.
It's a little worn, but I don't mind. I hope it won't
rain! I wish to-morrow was come!"

To-morrow came, and it didn't rain. Starting
after luncheon in the pony-carriage, Norah and her
father agreed that this was one of the days sent
expressly from Paradise for breakfasts, fêtes, pic-nics,
&c., but which so rarely reach their destination.

At Oakover everything seemed in holiday dress
for the occasion. The old trees towered in the full
luxuriance of summer foliage. The lawn, fresh
mown, smiled smooth and comely, like a clean-
shaved face. The stone balustrades and gravel
walks glared and glittered in the sun. The garden
was one blaze of flowers. Already a flapping
marquee was being pitched for refreshments, and
snowy bell-tents dotted the sward, for the different
purposes of marking scores, assorting prizes, and
carrying on flirtations. The targets, leaning back-
ward in jovial defiance, offered their round bluff

faces with an air that seemed to say " Hit me, if you
can !" and it is but justice to admit that, in one or
two instances, they had paid the penalty of their
daring with a flesh wound or so about the rims.

When Mr. Welby and his daughter arrived on
the ground, a few flights of arrows had already been
shot, and the archers were walking in bands to and
fro between the butts, with a solemnity that denoted
the grave nature of their pastime. Well might old
Froissart, on whose countrymen, indeed, a flight of
English arrows made no slight impression, describe
our people as " taking their pleasure sadly, after the
manner of their nation."

If there was one social duty which Mr. Vandeleur
fulfilled better than another, it was that of receiving
his guests. He had the knack of putting people at
ease from the outset. He made them feel they were
conferring a favour on himself by visiting his home,
while at the same time he preserved so much of
dignity and self-respect as conveyed the idea that
to confer favours on such a man was by no means
waste of courtesy. For Mr. Welby he had a cordial
greeting and a jest, for Norah a graceful compliment and a smile.

" The shooters have already begun, Miss Welby,"

said he, turning to welcome a fresh batch of guests; "and there's tea in the large tent. If you miss your chaperone at any time, you will be sure to find him in the library."

So Norah walked daintily on towards the targets, and many an eye followed her with approving glances as she passed. It is not every woman who can walk across a ball-room, a lawn, or such open space, unsupported, with dignity and ease. Miss Welby's undulating figure never looked so well as when thus seen aloof from others, moving smooth and stately, with a measured step and graceful bearing peculiarly her own. The smooth, elastic gait was doubtless the result of physical symmetry, but the inimitable charm of manner sprang from combined modesty and self-respect within.

Welby, a few paces behind, felt proud of his handsome daughter, looked it, and was not ashamed even to profess his admiration. There was a quaking heart all the time though under this attractive exterior. With one eager, restless glance Norah took in the whole company, and Gerard was not there. Worse still, Dolly Egremont had just made a "gold," and Dandy Burton was shooting aimlessly over the target.

Poor Norah began to be very unhappy. Luckily, however, she got hold of Lady Baker, and that welcome dowager, who was rather deaf, rather blind, and rather stupid, offered the best possible refuge till a fellow-pupil should come up to make his bow, and she might ask—in a roundabout way, be sure—what had become of Gerard Ainslie.

Mr. Archer's young gentlemen had hitherto taken advantage with considerable readiness of the very few opportunities that offered themselves to pay attention to Miss Welby. To-day, nevertheless, perverse fate decreed that both Egremont and Burton should be so interested in their shooting as to remain out of speaking distance. The Dandy, indeed, took his hat off with an elaborate flourish, but having been captured, in the body at least, by a young lady in pink, was unable, for the present, to do more than express with such mute homage his desire to lay himself at Miss Welby's feet.

It was weary work that waiting, waiting for the one dear face. Weary work to see everybody round her merry-making, and to be hungering still for the presence that would turn this penance into a holiday for herself as it was for the rest. There was always the hope that he might come late with Mr. Archer,

who had not appeared. And to so frail a strand
Norah clung more and more tenaciously as the day
went down, and this her last chance died out too.
Even Lady Baker remarked the worn, weary look
on that pale face, and proposed the usual remedy
for a heart-ache in polite circles, to go and have
some tea.

"This standing so long would founder a troop-
horse, my dear," said her ladyship. "Let's try for
a cup of tea. Mr. Vandeleur told me it was ready
two hours ago."

Norah assented willingly enough. He might be
in the tent after all, and for a while this spark of
hope kindled into flame, and then went out like
the rest.

In the tent, however, were collected the smartest
of the county people, including several young gentlemen professed admirers of Miss Welby. They
gathered round her the instant she appeared. Partly
yielding to the exigencies of society, partly to the
force of habit, partly to intense weariness and vexation, she joined in their talk, accepting the incense
offered her with a liveliness of tone and manner
betrayed for the first time to-day. Lady Baker
began to think her young friend was " rather giddy

for a clergyman's daughter, and a confirmed flirt,
like the rest of them."

And so the day wore on, and the shooters un-
strung their bows, making excuses for their ineffi-
ciency. Presently, the prizes were distributed, the
company adjourned into the house, rumours went
about of an *impromptu* dance, and people gathered in
knots, as if somewhat at a loss till it should begin.
Mr. Vandeleur moving from group to group, with
pleasant words and smiles, at last stopped by Norah,
and keeping on the deafest side of Lady Baker,
observed in a low tone—

"Your father is still wrestling hard with a Greek
misprint in the library. He won't want you to go
away for hours yet. We think of a little dancing,
Miss Welby; when would you like to begin?"

It was flattering to be thus made queen of the
revels; he meant it should be, and she felt it so.
Still she was rather glad that Lady Baker did not
hear. She was glad, too, that her host did not
secure her for the first quadrille, when she saw
Dandy Burton advancing with intention in his eye,
and she resolved to extract from that self-satisfied
young gentleman all the information for which she
pined.

Vandeleur had debated in his own mind whether
he should dance with her or not, but, having a
certain sense of the fitness of things, decided to
abstain.

"No! hang it!" he said to himself that morning
while shaving; "after a fellow's forty it's time
to shut up. I've had a queerish dance or two in
my day, and I can't complain. How I could open
their eyes here if I chose!" and he chuckled, that
unrepentant sinner, over sundry well-remembered
scenes of revelry and devilry in the wild wicked
times long ago.

The band struck up, the dancers paired, the set
was forming, and Burton, closely pursued by Dolly
Egremont, secured his partner.

"Too late!" exclaimed the triumphant cavalier
to his fellow-pupil. "Miss Welby's engaged.
Besides, Dolly, she considers you too fat to dance."

An indignant disclaimer from Miss Welby was lost
in Dolly's good-humoured rejoinder.

"You go for a waist, Dandy," said he, "and I
for a chest—that's all the difference. Besides, it's a
well-known fact that the stoutest men always dance
the lightest. You've got a square—Miss Welby
will, perhaps, give me the next round—

Turn, Fortune, turn thy wheel and lower the proud
Dandy! you dress too low, you dance too loud."

But Miss Welby was afraid she couldn't—didn't
think she should waltz at all—felt a little headache,
and wondered how Mr. Egremont could talk such
nonsense! Then she took her station by her partner,
and began. It was more difficult to pump the
Dandy than she expected. In the first place he
had thrown his whole mind into his costume, which,
indeed, it is but justice to admit, left nothing to be
desired; secondly, what little attention he might
otherwise have spared, was distracted by the uncon-
cealed admiration lavished on him by his *vis-à-vis*,
the young lady in pink; and, thirdly, his own idea
of conversation was a running fire of questions,
without waiting for answers, alternated by profuse
compliments, too personal to be quite agreeable.

"Don't you waltz, Miss Welby?" said he, the
instant they paused to allow of the side couples per-
forming the dignified motions they had themselves
executed. "You've got just the figure for waltz-
ing; I'm sure you must waltz well. Now I think
of it, I fancy I've seen you waltz with Gerard
Ainslie."

Perhaps he had. Perhaps that was the reason

she didn't waltz now. Perhaps she had made this absentee a promise that men selfishly exact, and even loving women accord rather unwillingly, never to waltz with anybody else. Perhaps a difference of opinion at a previous archery meeting of which we have heard may have arisen from a discussion on this very subject. I know not. At any rate, here was an opening, and Norah took advantage of it.

"He's a good waltzer—Mr. Ainslie," said she, drearily. "Why is he not here to-night?"

"Do you think he *is* quite a good waltzer?" asked her partner. "He dances smoothly enough, but don't you think he holds himself too stiff? And then, a fellow can't dance, you know, if—— It's your turn to go on!"

An untimely interruption, while she carried out a ridiculous pantomime with the gentleman opposite —a swing with both hands in the Dandy's—and a return to the previous question.

"You were going to tell me why Mr. Ainslie didn't come with you."

"I don't want to talk about Ainslie," answered the Dandy, with a killing smile. "I want to talk about yourself, Miss Welby. That's a charming

dress you've got on. I had no idea lilac could——
The others are waiting for us to begin."

And so the grand round came, and still Norah
had not extorted an answer to the question next her
heart. She looked paler and more dejected than
ever when her partner led her through the dancing-
room, proposing wine-and-water, ices, and such re-
storatives. She was very heart-sick and tired—tired
of the dancing, the music, the whole thing—not a
little tired of Dandy Burton himself and his plati-
tudes. Succour, however, was at hand. Vandeleur had
been watching her through the whole quadrille, only
waiting his opportunity. He pounced on it at once.

"You find the heat oppressive, Miss Welby," said
he, extricating her from Burton's arm, and offering
his own. "I never can keep this room cool enough.
Let me take you to the conservatory, where there is
plenty of air, and a fountain of water besides to
souse you if you turn faint."

It was a relief to hear his cheerful, manly tones
after the Dandy's vapid sentences. She took his
arm gratefully, and accompanied him, followed by
meaning glances from two or three observant ladies,
who would not have minded seeing their own
daughters in the same situation.

CHAPTER XII.

"This *is* delightful!" exclaimed Norah, drawing a full breath of the pure, cool night air, that played through the roomy conservatory, and looking round in admiration on the quaintly-twisted pillars, the inlaid pavement, the glittering fountain, and the painted lanterns hanging amongst broad-leafed tropical plants and gorgeous flowers. It seemed a different world from the ball-room, and would have been Paradise, if only Gerard had been there!

"I am glad *you* like it, Miss Welby," said Vandeleur, with a flattering emphasis on the pronoun. "Now sit down, while I get you some tea, and I'll give you leave to go and dance again directly I see more colour in your face. I take good care of you, don't I?"

" You do, indeed!" she answered gratefully, for
to the wounded, anxious heart there was something
both soothing and reassuring in the kindly manner
and frank, manly voice.

A certain latent energy, a suppressed power,
lurked about Vandeleur, essentially pleasing to
women, and Norah felt the influence of these male
qualities to their full extent while he brought her
the promised tea, disposed her chair out of the
draught, and seated himself by her side.

Then he led the conversation gradually to the
news she most desired to hear. It was Vandeleur's
habit to affect a good-humoured superiority in his
intercourse with young ladies, as of a man who was
so much their senior, that he might profess interest
without consequence and admiration without impertinence. Perhaps he found it answer. Perhaps,
after all, it was but the result of an inherent *bon-
hommie*, and a frankness bordering on eccentricity.
At any rate, he began in his usual strain—

" How kind of you, Miss Welby, to come and sit
quietly with an old gentleman in an ice-house
when you might be dancing forty miles an hour
with a young one in an oven. Dandy Burton,
or whatever his name is—the man with the shirt-

front—must hate me pretty cordially. That's another conquest, Miss Welby ; and so is his friend, the fat one. You spare none of us. Old and young ! No quarter. No forgiveness. Let me put your cup down ! "

" I like the fat one best," she answered, smiling, while she gave him her cup.

He moved away to place it in safety, and she did not fail to notice with gratitude that he kept his back turned while he proceeded :—

" The other's the flower of them all, Miss Welby, to my fancy, and I am very glad I was able to do him a turn. He got his commission, you know, the very day you left Marston. I should think he must have joined by now. I dare say he is hard at work at the goose-step already."

When he looked at her again, he could see by the way her whole face had brightened that she heard this intelligence for the first time. He observed, with inward satisfaction, that there could have been no interchange of correspondence ; and reflecting that young ladies seldom read the papers very diligently, or interest themselves in gazettes, was able to appreciate the value of the news he had just communicated.

Norah preserved her self-command as, whatever may be their weakness under physical pressure, the youngest and simplest woman can in a moral emergency. It was unspeakable relief to learn there was a reason for his past neglect and present non-appearance; but she felt on thorns of anxiety to hear where he had gone, what he was doing, when there would be a chance of seeing him again; and therefore she answered in a calm, cold voice that by no means deceived her companion—

"I never heard a word of it! I am very glad for Mr. Ainslie's sake. I believe he was exceedingly anxious to get his commission. Oh! Mr. Vandeleur, how kind of you to interest yourself about him!"

"We are all interested in him, I think, Miss Welby," he answered with a meaning smile. "I told you long ago I thought he had the makings of a man about him. Well, he has got a fair start. We won't lose sight of him, any of us; but you know he must follow up his profession."

She knew it too well, and would not have stood in the way of his success; no, not to have seen him every day, and all day long. And now, while she felt it might be years before they would meet again, there was yet a pleasure in talking of him, after the suspense and uncertainty of the last three days, that threw a reflected glow of interest even on the person to whom she could unbosom herself. Next to Gerard, though a long way off, and papa, of course, she felt she liked Mr. Vandeleur better than anybody.

He read her like a book, and continued to play the same game.

"I thought you would be pleased to know about him," said he, keeping his eyes, according to custom, averted from her face. "The others are all very well, but Ainslie is really a promising lad, and some day, Miss Welby, you and I will be proud of him. But he's only reached the foot of the ladder yet, and it takes a long time to get to the top. Come, Miss Welby, your tea has done you good. You're more like yourself again; and do you know that is a very becoming dress you have got on? I wish I was young enough to dance with you, but I'm not, so I'll watch you instead. It's no compliment to you to say you're very good to look at indeed."

"I am glad you think so," she answered, quitting his arm at the door of the dancing-room; and he fancied, though it was probably only fancy, that she had leaned heavier on it while they returned. At any rate, Vandeleur betook himself to the society of his other guests, by no means dissatisfied with the progress he had made.

And Norah embarked on the intricacies of the "Lancers," under the pilotage of Dolly Egremont, who contrived to make her laugh heartily more than once before the set was finished. She recovered her spirits rapidly. After all, was she not young, handsome, well-dressed, admired, and fond of dancing? She put off reflection, misgivings, sorrow, memories, and regrets, till the ball was over at least. Lady Baker, dull as she might be, was yet sufficiently a woman to notice the change in her young friend's demeanour, and having seen her come from the conservatory on their host's arm, not only drew her own conclusions, but confided them to her neighbour, Mrs. Brown.

"My dear," said her ladyship, "I've found out something. Mr. Vandeleur will marry again ;—you mark my words. And he's made his choice in this very room to-night."

Mrs. Brown, a lady of mature years, with rather a false smile, and very false teeth, showed the whole of them, well pleased, for she owned a marriageable daughter, at that moment flirting egregiously with Vandeleur, in the same room; but her face fell when Lady Baker, whose impartial obtuseness spared neither friend nor foe, continued in the same monotonous voice—

"He might do worse, and he might do better. He's done some foolish things in his life, and perhaps he thinks it's time to reform. I hope he will, I'm sure. She's giddy and flighty, no doubt; but I dare say it's the best thing for him, after all!"

Mrs. Brown assenting, began to have doubts about her daughter's chance.

"Who is it? and how d'ye know?" she demanded rather austerely, though in a guarded whisper.

"It's Norah Welby, and I heard him ask her," replied Lady Baker recklessly, and in an audible voice.

"Poor girl! I pity her!" said the other, touching her forehead, as she passed into the supper-room and commenced on cold chicken and tongue.

She pitied herself, poor Norah, an hour afterwards, looking blankly out from the brougham window on the dismal grey of the summer's morning. Papa was fast asleep in his corner, satisfied with his victory over the Greek particle, and thoroughly persuaded that his darling had enjoyed her dance. The pleasure, the excitement was over, and now the reaction had begun. It seemed so strange, so blank, so sad, to leave one of these festive gatherings, and not to have danced with Gerard, not even to have seen him; worse than all, to have no meeting in anticipation at which she could tell him how she had missed him, for which she could long and count the hours as she used to do when every minute brought it nearer yet. What was the use of counting hours now, when years would intervene before she should look on his frank young face, hear his kind, melodious voice? Her eyes filled and ran over, but papa was fast asleep, so what did it signify? She was so lonely, so miserable! In all the darkness there was but one spark of light, in all the sorrow but one grain of consolation. Strangely enough, or rather, perhaps, according to the laws of sympathy and the force of association, that light, that solace seemed to identify themselves with the presence and companionship of Mr. Vandeleur.

CHAPTER XIII.

FEW places could perhaps be less adapted for a private rehearsal than the staircase of a lodging-house in a provincial town ;—a provincial town enlivened only by a theatre open for six weeks of the year, and rejoicing in the occasional presence of the depôt from which a marching regiment on foreign service drew its supplies of men and officers. Nevertheless, this unpromising locality had been selected for the purpose of studying his part by an individual whose exterior denoted he could belong to no other profession than that of an actor. As the man stood gesticulating on the landing, he appeared unconscious of everything in the world but the character it was his purpose to assume. Fanny Draper, dodging out of a small, humbly-furnished bed-room, was somewhat startled by the energy with which this enthusiast threw himself at her feet, and seizing her hand in both his own, exclaimed with alarming vehemence—

"Adorable being, has not your heart long since apprised ye that Rinaldo is your devoted slave? He loves ye; he worships ye; he lives but in your glances; he dies beneath your—— "

"Lor, Mr. Bruff," exclaimed Fanny, "why, how you go on! I declare love-making seems never to be out of your head."

Mr. Bruff, thus adjured, rose, not very nimbly, to his feet, and assuming, with admirable versatility, what he believed to be the air of a man of consummate fashion, apologised for the eccentricity of his demeanour.

"Madam," said he, "I feel that on this, as on former occasions, your penetration will distinguish between the man and his professional avocations. I am now engrossed with the part of a lover in genteel comedy. My exterior will doubtless suggest to you that I am—eh? what shall I say?—not exactly disqualified for the character!"

Fanny glanced at his exterior—a square figure, a tightly-buttoned coat, a close-shaved face, marked with deep lines, and illumined by a prominent red nose.

She laughed and shook her head.

"Don't keep me long then, Mr. Bruff, and don't make love to me in earnest, please, more than·you can help."

While she spoke she looked anxiously along the passage, as though afraid of observation.

Mr. Bruff at once became Rinaldo to the core.

"Stand *there*, madam, I beg of you," said he. "A little farther off, if you please. Head turned somewhat away, and a softening glance. Could you manage a softening glance, do you think, when I come to the cue '*and dies beneath your scorn?*' Are you ready?" and Mr. Bruff plumped down on his knees once more to begin it all over again.

Fanny threw herself into the part. It was evidently not the first time that she had thus served as a lay-figure, so to speak, for the prosecution of Mr. Bruff's studies in his art. She sneered, she flouted, she bridled, she languished, and finally bent over his close-cropped head in an access of tenderness relieved by a flood of tears, with an air of passionate reality that, as Mr. Bruff observed while he wiped the dust from his trousers, and the perspiration from his face, was "more touching, and infinitely more true, than nature itself."

"You were born to be an actress," said he; "and I shall take care that you have box-orders every night while our company remains. It is a pleasure to know, even in such empty houses as these, that there is one person to whom a man can play and feel that his efforts are appreciated, and the niceties of his calling understood."

Then Mr. Bruff lifted his hat with an air combining, as he was persuaded, the roistering demeanour of professed libertinism with the dignity of a stage nobleman, *siècle Louis Quatorze*, and went his way rejoicing to the adjacent tavern.

Fanny must, indeed, have been a good actress. No sooner was he gone than her whole face fell, and on its fresh rosy beauty came that anxious look it is so painful to see in the countenances of the young, the look that is never there unless the conscience be ill at ease. The look of a wounded, weary spirit dissatisfied with itself. She waited on the landing for a minute or two, listening intently, then stole down-stairs, glided along the passage on tip-toe, and with a pale cheek and beating heart turned the handle of the sitting-room door.

The apartment was empty, and Fanny drew breath. On the table lay a letter that had arrived but a few minutes by the post. She pounced upon it, and fled upstairs as noiselessly, but far more quickly than she came down. Then she locked the door, and tore open the envelope with the cruel gesture of one who destroys some venomous or obnoxious reptile.

Had she been but half an hour later, had the post been delayed, had an accident happened to the mail-train, my story would never have been written. Ah! these little bits of paper, what destinies they carry about with them, under their trim envelopes and their demure, neatly-written addresses! We stick a penny stamp on their outside, and that modest insurance covers a freight that is sometimes worth more than all the gold and silver in the country. How we thirst for them to arrive! How blank our faces, and how dull our hearts, when they fail us! How bitter we are, how unkind and unjust towards the guiltless correspondent, whom we make answerable for a hundred possibilities of accident! And with what a reaction of tenderness returns the flow of an affection that has been thus obstructed for a day!

Fanny read the letter over more than once. The

first time her face took the leaden, ashy hue of the
dead ; but her courage seldom failed her long, either
for good or evil, and there was a very resolute look
about her eyes and mouth ere she was half-way
through the second perusal. Had it reached its
rightful owner, I think it would have been covered
with kisses and laid next to a warm, impulsive,
wayward, but loving heart. It was a production,
too, that might have been read aloud at Charing
Cross without prejudice to the writer's modesty and
fair fame. Here it is :—

"DEAR MR. AINSLIE,—I have to thank you for
your letter in papa's name and my own. He was
very much pleased to hear you had joined your
regiment, and we all wish you every success and
happiness in your new profession. We were disappointed not to see you before you left Mr. Archer,
who always speaks of you as his *favourite pupil ;*
and, indeed, I had no idea, when we went to London,
that you were going to leave our neighbourhood so
soon. We should certainly have put off our journey
for a day or two had we thought we were not even
to bid you good-bye. But you know you have our
very best wishes for your welfare. I will give your

message to papa, and shall be so glad to hear again if we can be of any service to you here. Even if you have nothing *very particular to say*, you may find time to send us a few lines. Your favourite roses are not yet faded, and I gathered some this morning, which are standing on my writing-table now. Good-bye, dear Mr. Ainslie. With kindest regards from us all, believe me ever

" Yours very truly,

" LEONORA WELBY."

"Marston Rectory, Sept. —th."

Then the last page was crossed (quite unnecessarily, for there was plenty of space below the signature) with two lines,—"I think I have written you a letter as correct and proper as your own, but I was *so* glad to get it all the same."

Fanny's smile was not pleasant when she concluded this harmless effusion. It deepened and hardened round her mouth, too, while she placed the letter . in an envelope, sealed it carefully, and directed it to John Vandeleur, Esq., Oakover, ——shire ; but it left her face very grave and sad, under a smart little bonnet and double black veil, while she walked stealthily to the post-office and dropped her missive in the box.

She had plenty of time to spare. Gerard was still in the little mess-room of the 250th Regiment, smoking a cigar, after the squad drill it was necessary he should undergo, and thinking of Norah, perhaps less than usual, because he was persuaded that his own letter must ere this have come to hand and that she would answer it at once.

He had joined his regiment, or rather its depôt, immediately on his appointment, without availing himself of the two months' leave indulgently granted by the Horse Guards on such occasions,—his great-uncle, an arbitrary and unreasonable old gentleman, having made this condition on purchasing the commission and outfit for his relative. Ainslie arrived in barracks consequently without uniforms, and without furniture, so he learned a good deal of his drill in a shooting-jacket; and as the depôt was on the eve of a march, took cheap lodgings in the neighbourhood, which he seldom visited but to dress for dinner and go to bed. He had led this life for some little time before he could summon up courage to write to Miss Welby, and he was now looking forward with a thrill of delight to finding her answer at his lodgings, when he returned, which he meant to do the moment he had finished his cigar.

The conversation of Ensign Ainslie and his comrades, I am bound to admit, was not instructive nor even amusing. They were smoking, and partaking also of soda-water strengthened by stimulants, in a bare, comfortless, little room, littered with newspapers, and redolent of tobacco, both stale and fresh. Time seemed to hang heavy on their hands. They lounged and straddled in every variety of attitude, on hard wooden chairs; and they spoke in every variety of tone, from the gruff bass of the red-faced veteran to the broken *falsetto* of the lately-joined recruit. A jaded mess-waiter, or a trim orderly-sergeant, appeared at intervals; but such interruptions in no way affected the flow of conversation, which turned on the personal charms of a lady, ascertained to have arrived lately in the town, and the mystery attached to her choice of residence.

Captain Hughes, a colonial lady-killer of much experience, expressed himself in terms of unqualified approval.

"The best-looking woman I've seen since we left Manchester," insisted the Captain, dogmatically. "I followed her all the way down Market Street, yesterday, and I give you my honour, sir, she's as straight on her ankles as an opera-dancer; with a figure—I haven't seen such a figure since I got my company. I'll tell you; she reminded me of 'the Slasher.' You remember 'the Slasher,' Jones? —girl that threw you over, last fall, so coolly, at Quebec."

Jones, a young warrior of fair complexion, and unobtrusive manners, owned that he had not forgotten; blushing the while uncomfortably, because that "the Slasher's" glances had wounded him in a vital place.

"I know where she lives, too," resumed the Captain, triumphantly. "I followed the trail, sir, like a Red Indian. Ah! they can't dodge a fellow that's had my practice in the game, even if they want to, which they don't. I'd two checks—one at a grocer's, and one at a glove-shop; but I ran her to ground at last."

"You'll tell *me!*" lisped little Baker, commonly called "Crumbs," the youngest of the party, senior only to Gerard in the regiment, but looking like a mere child by his side. "You'll tell *me*, of course, because I'm in your own Company. You can't get out of it; and we'll walk down this afternoon, and call together."

"Crumbs!" observed his captain, impressively, "you're the last man in the regiment I'd trust." (Crumbs looked immensely delighted). " Besides, you little beggar, you ought to be back at school ; and if I did my duty as the Captain of your Company, I'd make the Adjutant write to your mother and tell her so."

" Crumbs," no whit abashed, ordered a tumbler of brandy and soda as big as himself, from which he presently emerged, breathless, and observed, for anybody to take up—" Ainslie's cut you all out. He lodges in the same house ! "

Every eye was now turned on Ainslie, and Captain Hughes began to fear a rival in the line he had followed hitherto with such success. " I don't think it can be the same woman," said he, checking the mirth of the youngsters with a frown. " She lives in Ainslie's lodgings, I grant you, but she can only have come there yesterday, or I must have seen her before. Isn't it so, Ainslie ? "

" You know more about it than I do," answered the unconscious Gerard. " The only women I've seen in the house are Mother Briggs herself and a poor servant-girl they call H'Ann—very strong of the H. It must have been Mother Briggs you

followed home, Hughes. I'll congratulate her on
her conquest when I go back."

But Captain Hughes, nettled by loud shouts of
laughter, vigorously repudiated such an accusation,
and indeed seemed inclined to treat the matter
with some slight display of temper, when the
harmless Jones, who had been cooling his face by
looking out at window, changed the subject for
another almost equally congenial to his comrades.

"Bless'd if there isn't Snipe dismounting at the
gate!" he exclaimed joyfully; "there's a drummer
holding his nag. What a spicy chestnut it is!
Holloa, Snipy! come in, won't you, and have a
B. and S.?"

A voice was heard to reply in the affirmative;
and before the B. and S.—signifying a beaker of
brandy and soda-water—could make its appearance,
Mr. Snipe walked into the room, and sat himself
down amongst the officers with some little shame-
facedness, which he strove to conceal by squaring
his elbows, pulling down his shirt-cuffs, and coaxing
a luxuriant crop of brown whiskers under his chin.
Mr. Snipe was one of those enterprising individuals
who make a livelihood by riding steeplechases, and
are yet supposed by a pious fiction never to receive

money for thus exerting their energies and risking
their necks. Concerning Mr. Snipe's antecedents,
the officers of the 250th were pleasantly ignorant.
He had rented a farm, and failed. Had gone
into business as a horse-dealer, and failed. Had
been appointed to the Militia, but somehow never
joined his corps. Had been, ostensibly, in all
the good things of the Turf for the last three
years ; yet seemed to be none the richer, and none
the less hungry for a chance. Had been even
taken into partnership by a large cattle dealer,
when at his lowest ebb, and bought out of the
concern by his confiding principal before three
months expired. Mr. Snipe always said he was
too sharp for the business, and, I believe, his partner
thought so too. Since then he had been riding at
all weights, over all courses, wherever horses were
pitted against each other to gallop and jump, or to
be pulled and fall, as the case might be, and the
trainers' orders might direct. Mr. Snipe had figured
in France, in Germany, in Belgium, and once on a
thrice auspicious occasion had been within a stirrup
leather's thickness of winning the Liverpool ; that
is to say, but for its breaking he couldn't have
lost ! He seemed in easy circumstances for a con-

siderable period after this misfortune, smoked the best of cigars, and drank a pint of sherry every day, between luncheon and dinner-time.

This gentleman was a wiry, well-built, athletic man, somewhat below the middle size, but extremely strong for his weight. He could shoot, play rackets, whist, and cricket better than most people, and was a consummate horseman on any animal under any circumstances. His countenance, though good-looking, was not prepossessing; and his manners argued want of confidence, not so much in his impudence as in his social standing. What he might have been among ladies I am not prepared to say, but he seemed awkward and ill at ease even before such indulgent critics as the officers of the 250th Foot.

He carried it off, however, with a certain assumption of bravado, and entered the mess-room with that peculiar gait—half limp, half swagger—which it is impossible for any man to accomplish who does not spend the greatest part of his life in the saddle. Captain Hughes, as possessing an animal of his own in training, treated him with considerable deference; while the younger officers, including Jones, gazed on him with an admiration almost sublime in its intensity.

"How's the horse?" said this worthy, addressing himself at once to the Captain, without taking any more notice of his entertainers than a down-cast, circular half-bow, to be divided amongst them; "how's 'Booby by Idle-boy?' You haven't scratched him, have ye, at the last minute? I tell ye, he'll carry all the money to-morrow; and he ought to be near winning, too—see if he won't!"

"The horse is doing good work," answered Hughes, delighted to be thus recognised in his double capacity of sportsman and dandy before all his young admirers. "I make no secrets about him. He galloped this morning with 'Fleur-de-Lys,' and he will run to-morrow strictly on the square."

Mr. Snipe shot a glance from his keen eye in the speaker's face, and looked down at his own boots again directly.

"Of course! of course!" he repeated; "and you can't get more than two to one about him, neither here nor in town. Who's to ride him, Captain? I suppose *you* couldn't get up at the weight?"

"Impossible," answered Hughes, complacently, and trying to look as if he had ever dreamt of such a thing. "My brother officer, Mr. Ainslie, has

promised to steer him for me to-morrow; and I
agree with you we have a very fair chance of
winning."

Gerard, thus distinguished, came forward from
the fire-place, and observed, modestly :

" I'll do my best; but you know, Hughes, I have
never ridden a hurdle-race in my life."

Mr. Snipe's little red betting-book was half-way
out of his pocket, but at this candid avowal he
thrust it back again unopened. His quick eye had
taken in Gerard's active figure and frank, fearless
face, without seeming to be lifted from the ground;
and he knew how dangerous, on a good horse, was
an inexperienced performer, who would go away
in front. On second thoughts, however, he drew it
out once more; and taking a pull at his brandy and
soda, asked, in a very business-like tone—

" What will anybody lay me against 'Lothario?'
I'll take six to one he's placed. First, second, or
third—1, 2, 3, or a win. Come! he's as slow as a
mile-stone, but he can *stay* for a week. I'll take
five if I ride him myself ! "

Then began a hubbub of voices, a production of
betting-books, and a confusion of tongues, in the
midst of which Gerard made his escape to his own

lodgings, and rushed to the table whereon he was
accustomed to find his letters. Something like a
pang of real physical pain shot through him to see
it bare, and for one moment he felt bitterly angry
in his disappointment. The next came a rush of
contending feelings—love, humiliation, mistrust,
despondency, and a morbid, unworthy desire that
she, too, might learn what it was to suffer the pain
she had chosen to inflict. Then his pride rose to
the rescue, and he resolved to leave off caring for
anything, take life as it came, and enjoy the material
pleasures of the present, unburdened by thought for
the future, still less (and again the pain shot through
him) haunted by memories of the past. Altogether
he was in a likely frame of mind, when fairly
mounted on "Booby by Idle-boy," to make the pace
very good before he was caught.

CHAPTER XIV.

THE humours and events of a remote country race-course would be interesting, I imagine, only to the most sporting readers ; and for such there is an ample supply provided in a periodical literature, exclusively devoted to those amusements or pursuits which many people make the chief business of life.

It is unnecessary, therefore, to dwell upon the various incidents of such a gathering : the feeble bustle at the railway station, the spurious excitement promoted by early beer at the hotel, the general stagnation in the streets, or the dreary appearance of that thinly-sprinkled meadow, which on all other days in the year was called the Cow-pasture, but on this occasion was entitled the Race-course. Let us rather take a peep at the horses themselves as they

are walked to and fro in a railed-off space, behind
a rough wooden edifice doing duty for a stand, and
judge with our own eyes of their claims to success.

There are four about to start for the hurdle race,
and two of these, "Tom-tit" and "The Conspirator,"
are so swaddled up in clothing, that nothing of them
is to be detected save some doubtful legs and two
long square tails. Their riders are drinking sherry,
with very pale faces, preparatory to "weighing in ;"
and it is remarkable that their noses borrow more
colour from the generous fluid than their cheeks.
Notwithstanding so re-assuring an employment, they
have little confidence in themselves or their horses.
They do not expect to win, and are not likely to be
disappointed ; for having heard great things of
"Booby by Idle-boy," and entertaining besides misgivings that Mr. Snipe would hardly have brought
"Lothario" all this distance for nothing, it has
dawned upon them that they had better have saved
their entrance-money. Besides, they have even now
seen some work-people putting up the hurdles, and
they wish they were well out of it altogether.

Mr. Snipe, on the contrary, clad in a knowing
great-coat, with goloshes over his neat racing boots,
and a heavy straight whip under his arm, walks into

the enclosure, accompanied by a friend as sharp-look-
ing as himself, with his usual downcast glances and
equestrian shamble, but with a confidence in his own
powers that it requires no sherry to fortify nor to
create. He superintends carefully the saddling and
bridling of Lothario, an attention the animal acknowledges by laid-back ears and a well-directed attempt
to kick his jockey in the stomach. Mr. Snipe grins
playfully. "If you was only as fond of me as I am
of you!" says he, between his teeth ; and taking his
friend's arm, whispers in his ear. The friend—
who looks like a gambling-house keeper out of employment—disappears, losing himself with marvellous
rapidity in the crowd beneath the stand.

And now Gerard, clad in boots and breeches of
considerable pretension, and attired in a green silk
jacket and white cap—the colours of Captain Hughes
—emerges from the weighing-shed, where he has
first pulled down the indispensable twelve stone ; and
surrounded by admiring brother officers, walks
daintily towards his horse. The young man's eye is
bright, and the colour stands in his cheek. He
means to win if he can, and is not the least nervous.
Captain Hughes, who thinks it looks correct to be on
extremely confidential terms, remains assiduously at

his elbow, and whispers instructions in his ear from time to time, as he has seen great noblemen at Ascot do by some celebrated jockey. "Don't disappoint the horse, Gerard," says he, one minute; "Perhaps you'd better wait on Lothario, and come when you see Snipe begin," the next ; with various other directions of a contradictory nature, to each of which Gerard contents himself by answering, "All right !" meaning religiously to do his very best for the race.

But if the rider's nerves are unshaken by the prospect of a struggle for victory, as much cannot be said for the horse. "Booby by Idle-boy" is not quite thorough-bred, but has, nevertheless, been put through so severe a preparation that it might have served to disgust an "Eclipse." In the language of the stable, he has been "trained to fiddle-strings ; " and neither courage nor temper are the better for the ordeal. His skin looks smooth, but his flanks are hollow ; his eye is excited, his ears are restless ; he champs and churns at his bridle till the foam stands thickly on the bit ; he winces at the slightest movement, and betrays altogether an irritable desire to be off, and get the whole thing over, that argues ill for success.

Mr. Snipe, sitting at his ease on Lothario, watches

his adversary, swung by a soldier-servant into the saddle.

" I'm blessed if the young 'un isn't a workman ! " he mutters, while he marks Gerard's easy seat, and the light touch with which one hand fingers the rein, while the other wanders caressingly over the horse's neck; but his quick eye has already marked that the Booby's curb-chain is somewhat tight, and sidling up just out of kicking distance, Mr. Snipe renews his offer to take five to one about " his own brute," observing that " it is a sporting bet, for he does not really believe Lothario has the ghost of a chance ! "

Gerard declines, however ; alleging that he is only there to ride, and knows nothing about the merits of the horses, while he turns Booby out of the enclosure, and sends him for a " spin" down the course, followed by the others, with the exception of Mr. Snipe, who contents himself with a mild, shuffling little apology for a trot, that by no means enhances Lothario's character amongst the spectators.

They are much more pleased with the " Booby by Idle-boy," who goes raking down the meadow, reaching wildly at his bridle, and givingthe rider a great deal of unnecessary trouble to steady and

keep his head in the right place. Gerard handles
him with great skill, and pulling up opposite the
stand, receives yet further instructions from Captain
Hughes, who has already got his glasses out of
their case.

"Don't disappoint him, Gerard!" he reiterates
loudly, looking round the while for the applause he
considers his due. "Make the pace as good as you
can! Come away with him in front, and win as you
like!"

Mr. Snipe here telegraphs a nod to his friend
under the stand, and that speculator, after a few
hurried words with a respectable farmer and an
officer of the 250th, takes a pencil from his mouth
and writes something down in a little red book.

The Starter, a neighbouring Master of Harriers,
already brandishes a flag in his hand. Let us go
up into the stand, and witness the race from that
convenient vantage-ground.

A very well-dressed woman, with a black veil over
her face so thickly doubled as to serve for a mask,
is looking on with considerable interest, and whisper-
ing an observation from time to time in the ear of
her cavalier—a close-shaven man, with a prominent
red nose. She is evidently nervous, and crushes into

illegible creases the printed card she holds in her
hand. Mr. Bruff, on the contrary—for it is that
celebrated actor who has taken on himself the pleasing task of attending Fanny Draper to the races—is
minutely observant of the demeanour affected by
those who ride. His manager meditates bringing
out a piece of his own writing, under the title of
" Fickle Fortune ; or, the Gentleman Jockey," and
Mr. Bruff cannot suffer such an opportunity as the
present to go by unimproved. Every turn of Mr.
Snipe's body, every inflection of his somewhat unpleasant voice, is a lesson for the actor in the leading
character he hopes hereafter to assume.

Fanny gazes at Gerard with all her eyes. There is
something very romantic and captivating to her ill-
regulated mind in the terms on which they stand.
She is concerned in an intrigue of which he is the
principal object ; she is living, unknown to him,
in the same house ; she is watching his actions, and,
above all, his correspondence, every hour of the day ;
and she is doing her best and *wickedest* to detach
him from the woman he loves. There is a horrible
fascination in all this, no doubt; and then, how well
he looks in his silk jacket !

" He's a handsome fellow, too, isn't he, that one

in green?" she whispers to Mr. Bruff. "I hope
he'll win, I'm sure—and I think he must!"

"He's well made-up," answers her companion,
absently; "but he don't look the part like the quiet
one. I see how it's done!: A meaning expression
throughout; a glance that nothing escapes; a flash
at intervals, but the general tone very much kept
down. It's original business. It's striking out a
new line altogether. I think it ought to suit
me!"

Fanny turns very pale.

"Bother!" says she. "They're off!"

So they are. After several false starts, occasioned
I am bound to admit by the perverseness of Mr.
Snipe, and which nearly drive "The Booby" mad,
while they elicit much bad language and a threat
of complaint to the Stewards from the Master of
Harriers, who is accustomed to have things his own
way, the four horses get off, and bound lightly over
the first flight of hurdles, with no more interesting
result than that Conspirator nearly unships his rider,
and the jockey of Tom-tit loses his cap. Then,
keeping pretty close together, they come round the
far-end of the meadow at a pace more than usually
merry for the commencement of a race, due to the

violence of the Booby, increased by Lothario's proximity at his quarters.

And now they reach the second leap. Tom-tit, following the others, jumps it like a deer, but his jockey tumbles off, and lies for a moment motionless, as if he was hurt.

Fanny begins to think it dangerous, and averts her eyes.

"Is green still leading?" she asks in a faint voice.

"Green still leading!" echoes Mr. Bruff; but he is thinking less of the sport than of a peculiar twist in Mr. Snipe's features as he inspected the saddling of his horse before the start.

And now Conspirator is also out of the race, and the struggle is between Lothario and The Booby as they approach the last flight of hurdles. Fanny cannot resist raising her head to look, but she is horribly frightened. Gerard gathers his horse very skilfully for the effort, but The Booby, besides being fractious, is also blown. Mr. Snipe, too, on Lothario, has now come alongside, and without actually jostling him, edges his own horse, which is in perfect command, near enough to his adversary's to discompose him very much in his take-off. The Booby, giving his head a frantic shake, sticks his nose in the air and

refuses to be pacified. Gerard is only aware that
his horse is out of his hand, that the animal has
disappeared somehow between its rider's legs, that a
green wall of turf rises perpendicularly in his face,
that nose, mouth, and eyes are filled with a sweet,
yet acrid fluid, and that he is swallowed up alive in
a heaving, rolling, earthy, and tenacious embrace.

What Fanny saw was a shower of splintered wood
flying into the air, a horse's belly and girths, with
four kicking legs striking convulsively upward, and
a green jacket motionless on the sward, shut in, ere
she could breathe, by a swarm of dark, shifting
figures, increasing in an instant to a crowd.

She was not afraid *now.* "Mr. Bruff!" exclaimed
the girl, clutching his arm in a vice, and turning on
him a white face and a pair of shining eyes that
scared even the actor, "bring the fly down *there*—
quick! He musn't lie on the damp earth. Don't
stop me. Before I get to him he might——"

She choked, without finishing her sentence, but
she was out of the stand like a lapwing, while Mr.
Bruff, with almost equal alacrity, went to fetch the
fly.

He could not but observe, however, that Mr. Snipe,
returning to weigh after an easy victory, nodded his

head to his confederate with a gesture that was worth rounds of applause. He overheard, too, a remark that accompanied the action—

"You may bid them a hundred-and-fifty for the Booby, if you can't get him for less. He'd have landed it if he'd been properly ridden, I'll lay two to one!"

CHAPTER XV.

"THE WHITE WITCH."

"It was a pity," said half the county, that Mr. Vandeleur "gave so little" at Oakover. Never was a place more adapted for out-of-door gatherings, having for their object the wearing of becoming dresses and the general discomfiture of the male sex. There were walks within half a mile of the house, along which it was impossible to stroll in safety with a fair companion under a summer sun. There were pheasant-houses to go and see, standing apart in convenient nooks and shaded recesses. There was a little lake, and on its surface floated a little skiff calculated to hold only two people at a time. Above all, there was the spring of ice-cold water under the hill in the deer-park, that was obviously a special provision of nature for the promotion of pic-nics.

It is one of the last fine days of a summer that has lingered on into the early autumn. The blue sky is laced with strips of motionless white cloud. The sward is burnished and slippery with long-continued drought. Not a blade of arid grass, not a leaf of feathery, yellowing fern stirs in the warm, still, sunny atmosphere. Gigantic elms stand out in masses of foliage almost black with the luxuriance of a prime that is just upon the turn; and from their fastnesses the wood-pigeon pours its drowsy plaint—now far, now near, in all its repetitions suggestive still of touching memories, not unpleasing languor, and melancholy repose. The deer have retired to the farthest extremity of their haunts, scared, it would seem, by the white legs of two Oakover footmen, moving under an old elm, unpacking sundry hampers, and laying a large tablecloth on the grass beneath its shade. Vandeleur understands comfort, and with him a pic-nic simply means the best possible cold dinner that can be provided by a French cook, laid out by servants well-drilled in all the minute observances of a great house. To-day he has a gathering of his neighbours for the express purpose of eating and drinking in the deer-park instead of the dining-room. He is coming up the hill now, walking slowly with a lady on his arm, and followed by a pony-carriage, a barouche, and his own mail-phaeton, all freighted with guests who prefer a drive to a half-mile walk, on so broiling a day. The lady who has taken her host's arm for the short ascent at the end of their journey is dressed, as usual, in pink. Miss Tregunter has been told by a gentleman now present that no colour suits her so well. Consequently she is pink all over — pink dress, pink bonnet, pink ribbons, pink checks. " 'Pon my soul!" says Vandeleur, "you look like a picotee! I haven't such a flower in the garden. I wonder whether you'd bear transplanting!" Miss Tregunter, conscious that such a remark, though it would almost amount to an offer from anybody else, is only "Mr. Vandeleur's way," laughs and blushes, and puts her pretty pink parasol down to hide her pretty pink face.

Dolly Egremont, in the pony-carriage with Miss Welby, begins to fidget; and Dandy Burton wishes he had put on the other neckcloth—the violet one.

These two young gentlemen have nearly completed the term of their studies with Mr. Archer. Stimulated by Gerard's appointment, and fired with

noble emulation, they anticipate the dreaded ordeal
of examination next week not without misgivings,
yet devoutly hope it may be their luck to scrape
through.

Miss Welby looks very pretty, not only in the
eyes of her father behind in the barouche—and
persuaded but this very morning, with a great deal of
coaxing, to join the party—but in the opinion of
every other gentleman present; nay, even the
ladies, though they protest she is not "their style,"
cannot but admit that "the girl has some good
points about her, and would not be amiss if she
didn't look so dreadfully pale, and had a little more
colouring in her dress."

Norah does look pale, and quiet as is her costume,
it shows more colour than her cheek. Truth to tell,
Miss Welby is very unhappy. Day after day she
has been expecting an answer from Gerard to her
kind, playful, and affectionate letter, but day after
day she has been disappointed. Her heart sinks
when she reflects that he may be ill—that something dreadful may have happened to him, and
she knows nothing about it; worse still, that he
may have ceased to care for her, and what is there
left then? It galls and shames her to believe that

he has used her badly; and were he present, she
might have courage to show she was offended; but
he is far away, and what is the use of pride or
pique? What is the use of anything? It seems
such a mockery to have the homage of every one
else and to miss the only eye from which an admiring
glance would be welcome; the only voice from
which one word of approval would thrill direct to
her heart.

She has selected Dolly for her companion in the
pony-carriage because she cherishes some vague
idea that Gerard liked him better than the others;
but Dolly is unworthy of his good fortune, having
eyes at present only for Miss Tregunter, whom in
her pink dress this young gentleman considers
perfectly irresistible.

The rest of the party are paired off rather by
chance than inclination. Dandy Burton has found
himself placed side by side with Lady Baker, and
feels thankful that their short drive will so soon
be over, and he can select a more congenial companion for the rest of the afternoon.

Vandeleur, a thorough man of the world, and
when once started quite in his element on these
occasions, believes that he has now paid sufficient

attention to Miss Tregunter, who, being an heiress, is supposed to exact a little more homage than worse portioned damsels, and seeks for the face that has begun to haunt him strangely of late—in his business, in his pleasures, in his solitary walks, even in his dreams. That face looks pale, unhappy, and a little bored, so the Squire of Oakover resolves to bide his time. He has played the game too often not to know its niceties, and he is well aware that if a woman feels wearied while in a man's society, she unreasonably connects the weariness ever afterwards with the companion, rather than the cause. In the two or three glances he steals at her, she seems to him lovelier, more interesting, more bewitching than ever. Happiness is to most faces a wonderful beautifier; but there are people who look their best when they are wretched; and Norah Welby is one of them.

Vandeleur turns away to his other guests with a strange gnawing pain at his heart, that he never expected to feel again. It reminds him of the old times, twenty years ago; and he laughs bitterly to think that wicked, and worn, and weary as he is, there should still be room in his evil breast for the sorrow that aches, and rankles, and festers,

that according to a man's nature exalts him to
the highest standard of good, or sinks him to the
lowest degradation of evil. Twenty years ago, too,
he knows he was better than he is now. Twenty
years ago he might have sacrificed his own feelings
to the happiness of a woman he loved. But life
is short; it is too late for such childishness now.

"Burton, take off those smart gloves, and cut
into the pie. Miss Tregunter, come a little more
this way, and you will be out of the sun. Lady
Baker, I ordered that shawl expressly for you to
sit upon. Never mind the salad, Welby; they'll
mix it behind the scenes. Champagne—yes!
There's claret-cup and Badminton, if you like it
better. Mr. Egremont, I hope you are taking care
of Miss Welby."

Dolly, still uneasy about the pink young lady
opposite, heaps his neighbour's plate with food, and
fills her glass with champagne. Miss Welby looks
more bored than ever, and Vandeleur begins to
fear his pic-nic will turn out a failure after all.

The Dandy, seldom to be counted on in an emer-
gency, advances, however, boldly to the rescue.
He helps everybody round him to meat and drink.
He compliments Miss Tregunter on her dress; Miss

Welby, who eats nothing, on her appetite; and Lady Baker, who drinks a good deal, on her brooch. Then it is discovered that he can spin forks on a champagne-cork; and by degrees people begin to get sociable, glasses are emptied, tongues loosened, and the deer, feeding half a mile off, raise their heads in astonishment at the babble of the human voice.

Presently somebody wants to smoke. It is not exactly clear with whom this audacious proposal originates, but Dandy Burton declares stoutly in favour of the movement. Lady Baker, whom every one seems tacitly to suspect as a dissentient, has no objection, provided her glass is once more filled with champagne. She even hazards an opinion that it will keep off the flies. Miss Tregunter would like to smoke, too, only she knows it would make her head ache, and fears it might have results even more unpleasant than pain. By the time the cigars are well under way, silence seems to have settled once more upon the party, but it is the silence of repose and contentment, rather than of shyness and constraint.

Miss Welby, awaking from a profound fit of abstraction, asks in a tone of injured feeling, "Why does nobody sing a song?"

"Why, indeed?" says Vandeleur. "If I had ever done such a thing in my life, I would now. Miss Tregunter, I know you can pipe more sweetly than the nightingale—won't you strike up?"

"No, I won't strike up, as you call it," answered Miss Tregunter, laughing; "my poor little pipe would be lost in this wilderness. Nothing but a man's voice will go down in the open air. Mr. Burton, I call upon you to begin."

But the Dandy could not sing without his music, nor, indeed, was he a very efficient performer at any time, although he could get through one or two pieces creditably enough in a room, with somebody who understood his voice to play the accompaniment, and everything else in his favour. He excused himself, therefore, looking imploringly at Dolly the while.

Miss Tregunter followed his glance. "You'll sing, I'm sure, Mr. Egremont," she said, rather affectionately. "I know you can, for everybody says so; and it seems so odd that I should never have heard you!"

Dolly, like all stout men, had a voice. Like all stout men, too, he was thoroughly good-natured; so he would probably have complied at any rate, but there was no resisting such an appeal, from such a quarter. He looked admiringly in the young lady's face.

"Willingly," said he. "What shall I sing?"

"'Rule Britannia,'" observed Norah, listlessly, and with a curl of her lip, sufficiently ungrateful to the willing performer.

"No, no!" protested Miss Tregunter. "How can you, dear?"

"Well, 'God save the Queen,' then," suggested Miss Welby, who was obviously not in a good humour.

"That always comes at the finish," said Burton. "Don't be sat upon, Dolly. Put your other pipe out, and sing us the 'White Witch.'"

"Why the 'White Witch?'" asked Vandeleur. "It sounds a queer name. What does it mean?"

"It don't mean anything," answered Dolly. "It's a song Gerard brought down from London before he went away. He was always humming it—very much out of tune. He said it reminded him of somebody he knew. Very likely his grand-mother!"

Norah Welby blushed scarlet, and then turned pale. Nobody observed her but Vandeleur; and

his own brow darkened a good deal. " Let us have
it by all means! " he said, with admirable self-
command, at the same time stretching forward to
fill his glass, and thus screening Miss Welby from
observation.

Dolly now struck up in a full mellow voice—

" Have a care ! She is fair,
  The White Witch there,
In her crystal cave, up a jewelled stair.
She has spells for the living would waken the dead,
And they lurk in the line of her lip so red,
And they lurk in the turn of her delicate head,
  And the golden gleam on her hair.

" Forbear ! Have a care
  Of her beauty so rare,
Of the pale proud face, and the queen-like air,
And the love-lighted glances that deepen and shine,
And the coil of bright tresses that glisten and twine,
And the whispers that madden—like kisses, or wine.
  Too late ! Too late to beware.

" Never heed ! Never spare !
  Never fear ! Never care !
It is better to love, it is bolder to dare.
Lonely and longing and looking for you,
She has woven the meshes you cannot break through,
She has taken your heart, you may follow it too.
  Up the jewelled stair, good luck to you there !
  In the crystal cave, with the witch so fair,
  The White Witch fond and fair."

" A bad imitation of Tennyson," remarked Vande-

leur. "But well sung, Mr. Egremont, for all that.
I am sure we are very much obliged to you."

"I know I am," said Miss Tregunter; at which
Dolly looked extremely gratified. "I am glad I
have heard you sing, and I should like to hear
you again."

"It's certainly pretty!" affirmed Lady Baker,
drowsily. "What is it all about?"

Norah's eyes looked very deep and dark, shining
out of her pale face. "I should like to have that
song," said she, in a low voice. "Mr. Egremont,
will you copy it out, and send it me?"

Vandeleur flung the end of his cigar away with
a gesture of impatience, even of irritation. "Poor
Ainslie!" said he, in a marked tone; "I wish he
hadn't left Archer's quite so soon."

"Have you heard anything of him?" asked Dolly,
eagerly. "The place hasn't been the same since
he went away. A better chap never stepped than
Ainslie. I'm sure I wish he was back again."

Alas, that on this young gentleman's preoccupied
heart the kindly glance that Norah now vouchsafed him should have been so completely thrown
away!

"I've heard no good of him," answered Vandeleur, gravely. " Young fellows are all wild ; and I'm the last man to object, but our friend has been doing the thing a little too unscrupulously, and I, for one, am very sorry for it."

"He always wanted knowledge of the world," observed Burton, in a tone of considerable self-satisfaction. " I knew he would come to grief, if they let him run alone too soon."

" I'll swear he's never done anything really wrong or dishonourable ! " protested Dolly, in a great heat and fuss, which surrounded him as with a glory in the eyes of Miss Welby. " I believe Gerard Ainslie to be the most perfect gentleman in the world ! "

" I believe you to be the most perfectly good-natured fellow I know," answered Vandeleur, laughing. " Come, it's cooler now, shall we take a stroll in the Park ? By-the-bye, Miss Welby, I haven't forgotten my promise to show you the Rock House."

Miss Welby's proud pale face grew prouder and paler as she bowed assent, and walked off with her host in the direction indicated. Vexed, wounded, and justly irritated, she could not yet resist the temptation of trying to learn something definite concerning Gerard Ainslie.

CHAPTER XVI.

PIOUS ÆNEAS.

"I'M bored about a friend of ours, Miss Welby," observed Vandeleur, preceding his guest along a narrow path through the fern, out of hearing by the other, and careful not to look back in her face. "This way, and mind those brambles don't catch in your pretty dress. It isn't often I allow anything to vex me, but I am vexed with young Ainslie. I thought him such a nice, straightforward, well-disposed boy; and above all, a thorough gentleman. It only shows how one can be deceived."

She felt her cheek turn white and her heart stand still, but her courage rose at the implied imputation, and she answered boldly: "Whatever may be Mr. Ainslie's faults, he is the last person in the world I should suspect of anything false or un-gentlemanlike."

"Exactly what I have said all along," assented
Vandeleur; "and even now I can scarcely bring
myself to believe in the mischief I hear about him,
though I grieve to say I have my information from
the best authority."

She stopped short, and he turned to look at her.
Vandeleur had often admired a certain dignity and
even haughtiness of bearing which was natural to
Norah. He had never seen her look so queen-like
and defiant as now.

"Why don't you speak out, Mr. Vandeleur?"
she said, somewhat contemptuously; "I am not
ashamed to own that I do take an interest in Mr.
Ainslie. It would be strange if I did not, considering that he is a great friend of papa's, as well as
mine. If you know anything about him, why don't
you proclaim it at once?"

He dropped his voice and came closer to her side.
"Shall I tell you why I don't?" said he, tenderly.
"Because I'm soft; because I'm stupid; because
I'm an old fool. Miss Welby, I would rather cut
my right hand off than give you a moment's pain;
and I know your heart is so kind and good that it
would pain you to hear what I have learned about
Gerard Ainslie."

"You have no right to say so!" she burst out, vehemently, but checked herself on the instant. "I mean you cannot suppose that it would pain me more than any of his other friends to hear that he was doing badly. Of course, I should be very sorry," she added, trying to control her voice, which shook provokingly. "Oh, Mr. Vandeleur! after all he's very young, and he's got nobody to advise him. Can't you help him? Can't you do something? What is the matter? What has he really been about?"

"I scarcely know how to tell you," he answered, shaking his head with an admirable assumption of consideration and forbearance. "There are certain scrapes out of which a young fellow may be pulled, however deeply he is immersed, if he will only take advice. I've been in hundreds of them myself. But this is a different business altogether. I've gone through the whole thing, Miss Welby. Heaven forbid you should ever learn one-tenth of the sorrows and the troubles and the evils that beset a man's entrance on life! I have bought my experience dearly enough;—with money, with anxiety, with years of penitence and remorse. People will tell you that John Vandeleur has done everything, and been through everything, and got tired of everything. People will tell you a great deal about John Vandeleur that isn't true. Sometimes I wish it was! Sometimes I wish I could be the hard, heartless, impenetrable, old reprobate they make me out. However, that's got nothing to do with it. All I say is, that even with my experience of evil I don't know what to advise."

"Is it money?" she asked; but her very lips were white, and her voice sank to a whisper.

"Far worse than that!" he exclaimed. "If it had been only an affair of extravagance, it would never have come to your ears, you may be sure! After all, I like the lad immensely, and I would have persuaded him to allow me to arrange any-thing of that kind in ten minutes. No, Miss Welby, it is not money; and not being money, can you guess what it is?"

Of course she could guess! Of course she had guessed long ago! Of course the jealousy insepa-rable from love had given her many a painful twinge during the last half hour; and equally, of course, she affected innocence, ignorance, profound indifference, and answered never a word.

He looked designedly away, and she was grateful for his forbearance. "Not being money," he continued, "we all know it must be love. And yet I cannot call this unaccountable, this incomprehensible infatuation, by so exalted a name. I tell you the whole thing beats me from beginning to end. Here was a young man with every advantage of education and standing and society, thrown amongst the nicest people in the neighbourhood, visiting at several of our houses, and popular with us all;—a young man who, if he was like young men in general, ought to have been doubly and triply guarded against anything in the shape of folly or vice; who should have been under an influence the most likely to keep him pure, stainless, and unselfish; an influence that preserves almost all others, even old sinners like myself, from the very inclination to evil. And on the threshold of life he casts away every advantage; he sets propriety at defiance; he outrages the common decencies of the world, and he hampers himself with——Miss Welby, I ought not to go on—I ought never to have begun. This is a subject on which it is hardly fit for you and me to converse. See how well the house comes in from here; and give me your advice about taking out that dwarfed oak ; it hides more than half the conservatory."

She could see neither dwarfed oak nor conservatory, for her eyes were beginning to cloud with tears, bravely and fiercely kept back. But she had not reached the ordeal thus designedly to shrink from it at last; and though she spoke very fast, every syllable was clear and distinct while she urged him to proceed.

"Tell me the whole truth, Mr. Vandeleur, and nothing but the truth. I have a right to ask you. I have a right to know everything."

So pale, so resolute, and so delicately beautiful ! For a moment his heart smote him hard. For a moment he could have spared her, and loved her well enough to make her happy, but even in his admiration his lower nature, never kept down for years, gained the mastery, and he resolved that for her very perfection she must be his own. Again he turned his head away and walked on in front.

"I will tell you the truth," he said, with a world of sympathy and kindness in his voice. "Ainslie has been worse than foolish. He has been utterly dishonourable and unprincipled. He has taken a young girl of this neighbourhood away from her

home. They are together at this moment. You
know her, Miss Welby. She is old Draper's
daughter, at Ripley Mill. Come into the Rock
House, and sit down. Is it not delightfully cool?
Wait here half a minute, and I will bring you the
purest water you ever tasted, from the spring at the
foot of those steps."

He was out of sight almost while he spoke, and
she leaned her head against the cold slab which
formed part of the grotto they had entered, feeling
grateful for the physical comfort it afforded to sink
into a seat and rest her aching temples even on a
stone.

It was over then—all over now! Just as she suspected throughout, and she had been right after all.
Then came the dull sense of relief that in its hopelessness is so much worse to bear than pain; and
she could tell herself that she had become resigned,
careless, stupefied, and hard as the rock against
which she leaned her head. When Vandeleur came
back, she looked perfectly tranquil and composed.
Impenetrable, perhaps, and haughtier than he had
ever seen her, but for all that so calm and self-
possessed that she deceived even him. "She cannot have cared so much, after all," thought

Vandeleur; "and there is a good chance for me still."

He offered her some water, and she noticed the quaint fashion of the silver cup in his hand.

"What a dear old goblet," she said, spelling out the device that girdled it in ancient characters, almost illegible. "Do you mean to say you leave it littering about here?"

He smiled meaningly. "I sent it up on purpose for you to drink from. There is a story about the goblet, and a story about the Rock House. Can you make out the motto?"

"Well, it's not very plain," she answered; "but give me a little time. Yes. I have it—

> ' Spare youth,
> Have ruth,
> Tell truth.'

It sounds like nonsense. What does it mean?"

"It's a love story," replied Vandeleur, sitting down by her side, "and it's about my grandmother. Shall I tell it you?"

She laughed bitterly. "A love-story! That must be ludicrous. And about your grandmamma, Mr. Vandeleur! I suppose, then, it's perfectly proper. Yes. You may go on."

"She wasn't my grandmother then," said Vandeleur; "on the contrary, she had not long been my grandfather's wife. She was a good deal younger than her husband. Miss Welby, do you think a girl could care for a man twenty years older than herself?"

She was thinking of her false love. "Why not," she asked, "if he was staunch and true?"

Vandeleur looked pleased, and went on with his story:—

"My grandfather loved his young bride very dearly. It does not follow because there are lines on the forehead and silver streaks in the beard that the heart should have outlived its sympathies, its affections, its capability of self-sacrifice and self-devotion. It sounds ridiculous, I dare say, for people to talk about love when they are past forty, but you young ladies little know, Miss Welby; you little know. However, my grandfather, as old a man as I am now, worshipped the very ground his young wife trod on, and loved her no less passionately, and perhaps more faithfully, than if he had been five-and-twenty. She was proud of his devotion, and she admired his character, or she would not probably have married him; but her heart had been touched by a young cousin in the neighbourhood,—only scratched, I think, not wounded to hurt, you know,—and whatever she indulged in of romance and sentiment, was associated with this boy's curly locks, smooth face, and frivolous, empty character. There is a charm in youth, Miss Welby, I fear, for which truth, honour, station, and the purest affection are no equivalents."

She sighed, and shook her head. Vandeleur proceeded :—

" My grandfather felt he was not appreciated as he deserved, and it cut him to the heart. But he neither endeavoured to force his wife's inclinations nor watched her actions. One day, however, taking shelter from a shower under that yew-tree, he heard his wife and her cousin, who had been driven to the same refuge, conversing on the other side. He was obliged to listen, though every word spoken stabbed him like a knife. It was evident a strong flirtation existed between them. Nothing worse, I am bound to believe ; for in whose propriety shall a man have confidence, if not in his grandmother's ? Nevertheless, the hidden husband heard his wife tax her cousin with deceiving her, and the young man

excused himself on the grounds of his false position
as a lover without hope. This was so far satisfactory.
'And if your husband asked you whether you had
seen me to-day, what should you answer?' demanded
the cousin. 'I should tell him the truth,' replied
my grandmother. This was better still. The next
communication was not quite so pleasant for the
listener. His wife complained bitterly of the want
of shelter in this, the only spot, she said, where they
could meet without interruption; in rain, she protested, they must get drenched to the skin, and in
hot weather there was not even a cup to drink
out of from the spring. The cousin, on the other
hand, regretted loudly that his debts would drive
him from the country, that he must start in less
than a week, and that if he had but two hundred
pounds he would be the happiest man in the world.
Altogether it was obvious that the spirits of this
interesting couple fell rapidly with their pros-
pects.

"The rain fell too, but my grandfather was one of
the first gentlemen of his day, and notwithstanding
the ducking he got, walked away through the
heaviest of it, rather than remain for their leave-
taking. We are a wild race, we Vandeleurs, but

there is some little good in us if you can only get at it."

"I am sure there is," said she absently; "and, at least, you have none of you ever failed in loyalty."

"Thank you, Miss Welby," said Vandeleur,. now radiant. "'*Loyal je serais durant ma vie !*' Well, if you can stand any more about my grandmother, I will tell you exactly what happened. It rained for three days without intermission—it sometimes does in this country. During that period an unknown hand paid the cousin's debts, enabling him to remain at home as long as he thought proper ; and on the fourth morning, when the sun shone, my grandmother, taking her usual walk to the spring, found not only her cousin at the accustomed spot, but this Rock House erected to shelter her, and that silver cup ready to drink from, encircled, as you see it, with the motto you have just read. All these little matters were delicate attentions from a husband twenty years older than herself ! "

"He must have been a dear old thing ! " exclaimed Norah, vehemently. "Wasn't she delighted ? And didn't she grow awfully fond of him after all ?"

"I don't know," answered Vandeleur very gravely, and in a low voice that trembled a little. "But

I am sure if she did *not*, he was a miserable man for
his whole life. It is hard to give gold for silver,
as many of us do ungrudgingly and by handfuls;
but it is harder still to offer hopes, happiness—
past, present, future—your existence, your very soul,
and find it all in vain, because the only woman on
earth for *you* has wasted her priceless heart on an
object she knows to be unworthy. She gives her
gold for silver—nay, for copper; and your dia-
monds she scorns as dross. Never mind! Fling
them down before her just the same! Better that
they should be trodden under foot by her, than set
in a coronet for the brows of another! Miss Welby
—Norah! that is what I call *love!* An old man's
love, and therefore to be ridiculed and despised!"

She had shrunk away now, startled, scared by his
vehemence; but he took her hand, and continued
very gently, while he drew her imperceptibly towards him—

"Forgive me, Miss Welby—Norah! May I not
call you Norah? I have been hurried into a confes-
sion that I had resolved not to make for months—
nay, for years—perhaps not till too late even for
the chance of reaping anything from my temerity.
But it cannot be unsaid now. Listen. I have

loved you very dearly for long; so dearly that I
could even have yielded up my hopes without a
murmur, had I known your affections gained by
one really worthy of you, and could have been content with my own loneliness to see my idol happy.
Yes, I love you madly. Do not draw away from
me. I will never persecute you. I do not care
what becomes of me if I can only be sure that you
are contented. Miss Welby! I offer *all*, and I ask
for so little in return! Only let me watch over
your welfare, only let me contribute to your happiness; and if you can permit me to hope, say so;
if not, what does it matter? I shall always love
you, and belong to you—like some savage old dog,
who only acknowledges one owner—and you may
kick me, or caress me, as you please."

She was flattered—how could she be otherwise?
And it was a salve to her sore suffering heart to
have won so entirely the love of such a man—of
this distinguished, well-known, experienced Mr.
Vandeleur. As a triumph to her pride, no doubt
such a conquest was worth a whole college of
juveniles; and yet, soothed pique, gratified vanity,
budding ambition—all these are not love, nor are
they equivalents for love.

She knew it even at this moment; but it would have been heartless, she thought—ungrateful, unfeeling—to speak harshly to him now. She drew her hand away; but she answered in a low and rather tender voice, with a smile that did not in the least conceal her agitation—

" You are very noble and very generous. I could not have the heart to *kick* you, I am sure ! "

" And I may hope ? " he exclaimed, exultingly. But her face was now hidden, and she was crying in silence.

He was eager for an answer. He had played the game so well, he might consider it fairly won.

" One word, Miss Welby—Norah, my darling Norah ! I will wait any time —I will endure any trial—only tell me that it will come at last ! "

" Not yet," she whispered—" not yet ! "

And with this answer he was fain to content himself, for no farther syllable did Miss Welby utter the whole way down the hill, the whole way across the deer-park, the whole way along the half-mile avenue to the house. They reached it like strangers, they entered it at different doors, they mixed with the various guests as if they had not a thought nor an interest in common ; yet none the less did Norah Welby feel that, somehow against her will, she was fastened by a long and heavy chain, and that the other end was held by John Vandeleur, Esq., of Oakover.

CHAPTER XVII.

THE GIRLS WE LEAVE BEHIND US.

Mr. Bruff never sees his fellow-lodger now. If his enthusiasm for the profession impels him to impromptu rehearsals, they must be dependent on the good-nature of old mother Briggs, or the leisure moments, not easily arrested, of the hard-worked H'Ann! He is little impressed by female charms; for although, like actors in general, he looks of no particular age, and might be anything between thirty and sixty, Mr. Bruff has acquired that toughness of cuticle, both without and within, which defends the most sensitive of us after our fiftieth birthday; and impassioned as he may appear in the character of a stage lover, to use his own expression, he is " adamant, sir, adamant to the backbone!" in private life. Nevertheless, he con-

siders the young lady he has been in the habit
of meeting on the stairs "a very interesting party;"
and presiding as he does to-night at a late supper,
dramatic and convivial—the forerunner of speedy
departure to another provincial theatre—he finds
himself thinking more than once of Fanny Draper's
well-shaped figure, mobile features, bright eyes, and
pleasant saucy smile. He wonders who she is, and
what she is. He wonders, with her natural powers
of mimicry, with her flexibility of voice and facility
of expression, with her advantages of appearance
and manner, why she does not take to the profession,
and appear at once upon the stage. He wonders
(in the interval between a facetious toast and a comic
song) whether her residence in this dull provincial
town is not intimately connected with the presence
of that young officer in whose accident she took such
obvious interest; whether it is a case of thrilling
romance, fit subject for a stock-piece, or of mere
vulgar intrigue. He wonders why she has been
absent from the theatre; why she has returned him
the orders he sent her this very afternoon; why he
has not met her in the street or on the stairs; and
while he empties his glass and clears his voice for
the comic song, he wonders what she is doing now.

Fanny Draper is dreaming—dreaming broad
awake—buried in a deep, high-backed, white-
covered armchair, with her eyes fixed on the
glowing coals of a fire that she makes up from time
to time with noiseless dexterity, stealing anxious
glances the while towards the close-drawn curtains
of a large old-fashioned bed. It is long past
midnight. Not a sound is heard outside in the
deserted street, not a sound in the sick chamber,
but the measured ticking of a watch on the chimney-
piece. Throughout the room there is every appearance of dangerous illness combated with all the
appliances of medical skill and affectionate attention. There are towels baking on a screen within
reach of the fire-glow; layers of lint lie neatly
packed and folded on squares of oil-skin; long
bandages, dexterously rolled and tied, wait only to
be uncoiled with a touch; two or three phials,
marked in graduated scale, stand on the dressing-
table; a kettleful of water is ready to be placed
on the hob; and in a far-off corner, escaping from
the lowest drawer of the wardrobe, peeps out a
tell-tale cloth stained and saturated with blood.

In that close-curtained bed lies Gerard Ainslie
hovering between life and death. He has never

spoken since they lifted him from under his horse
on the race-course, and brought him home to his
lodgings, a crushed, mutilated form, scarcely breathing, and devoid of sight or sense. Mrs. Briggs
opines it is "all over with him, poor young man!
though while there's life there's hope o' coorse!"
and H'Ann has been in a chronic state of smuts
and tears since the day of the accident. But Fanny
constituted herself sick-nurse at once, and the doctor
has told her that if the patient recovers it will be
less owing to surgical skill than to her affectionate
care and self-devotion. He had better have held
his tongue. Poor girl! she never broke down till
then, but she went and cried in her own room for
forty minutes after this outburst of professional
approval.

If he recovers! Fanny has only lately learnt how
much that little word means to her,—how entirely
her own welfare depends on the life of this hapless
young gentleman, whom she once considered fair
game for the enterprise of a coquette, whom she
has been paid (how she winces with shame and pain
at the remembrance!)—yes, paid to captivate and
allure! It was a dangerous game; it was played
with edged tools; and not till too late for salve or

plaster did the miller's daughter find out that she had cut her own fingers to the bone. Now all she prizes and loves in the world lies senseless there within those close-drawn curtains; and her wilful heart has ceased beating more than once when, listening for the only sign of life the sufferer displayed, she fancied his breathing had stopped, and all was over.

To-day, however, there seemed to be a slight improvement, though imperceptible, save to the eye of science. The doctor's face (and be sure it was eagerly watched) had looked a shade less solemn, a thought more anxious. He was coming earlier, too, than usual on the morrow. And had he not said once before that any change would be for the better? Surely it is a good omen. For the first time since she has taken possession of that deep armchair by the fire in the sick chamber, Fanny suffers her thoughts to wander, and her spirit to lose itself in dreams.

She reviews her life since she has been here— the new existence, brightened by the new feeling which has taken possession of her, body and soul. Thanks to Mr. Bruff's kindness, she has been often to the theatre; and according to her natural ten-

dencies, has derived considerable gratification from
her visits. In the two or three pieces she has witnessed she can remember every character, almost
every line of every part. It seems so foolish, and
yet so natural, to identify the hero with Gerard, the
heroine with herself. When Mr. Bruff, as Rinaldo,
in a black wig, a black belt, a pair of black boots,
black moustaches, and enormous black eyebrows,
declared his love to Helena, no people could be
more different than that hoarse tragedian and slim,
soft-spoken Gerard Ainslie. Yet it seems to her now
that she was Helena, and Rinaldo was the young
officer. When Bernard, in the *Brigand's Bride*,
stuck a lighted candle into a barrel of gunpowder
(ingeniously represented by a bushel of dirty
flour), and dared his ruffian band, who "quailed,"
to use his own words, "before their captain's eye,"
to remain in circle round these combustibles, and
thus vindicate the claims of the boldest to the best
of the spoil—in this case consisting of the golden-
haired Volante, a princess in her own right, in-
curably in love with Bernard, of whom she was
supposed to know nothing but that he had set her
father's castle on fire, and carried her off by main
force as his captive;—why, I ask, should Fanny

Draper have longed to be placed in so false, not
to say so perilous a position, if only to be delivered
in the same uncomfortable manner by her own
ideal of a lawless brigand, carried out in the character of an ensign belonging to a marching regiment, lately joined, and not yet perfect in his drill?
Why, indeed! except that Fanny had fallen in love,
and was mistress neither of her thoughts, her feelings, nor her actions.

Had it been otherwise, she feels she might have
done good business since she came to this obscure
country town. She might have bettered her position, and, for a person of her station, made no small
progress up the social ladder, in all honour and
honesty. Not only on the stage has she lately
witnessed scenes of love-making and courtship.

Fixing her eyes on the gloomy coals, she beholds
again a drama in which but very lately she enacted
a real and an important part. She is walking down
the High Street once more, in a grey silk dress, with
a quiet bonnet, and lavender gloves, and a get-up
that she is well aware combines the good taste of
the lady with the attractions of the coquette. She
is overtaken by Captain Hughes, who professes a
surprise thus to meet her; the more remarkable

that at the close of their last interview something
very like a tacit agreement provided for their next
to be held in this very spot. He asks leave, demurely enough, to accompany her part of the way
during her walk; and when she accords permission,
she is somewhat startled to find the captain's usual
flow of conversation has completely failed him, and
he seems to have discovered something of engrossing
interest in the knot that fastens his sash. As the
experienced fisherman feels instinctively the rise
before he strikes, Fanny is as sure she has hooked
her captain as if he was gasping at her feet; and
is not the least surprised when he does speak, that
his voice comes thick and hoarse like that of a man
in liquor, or in love.

He tells her the day is fine, the weather is altered
for the better; that there is no parade at the barracks to-morrow; that the depôt is about to change
its quarters; that, for himself, he expects his orders
to join the service-companies forthwith; and then
—he stops, clears his throat, and looks like an
idiot!

"It's coming," thinks Miss Draper; but she
won't help him, and he has recourse to his sash once
more.

At last he gives a great gulp, and asks her to accompany him.

"He has watched her ever since she came. He has admired her from the first. He never saw such a girl before. She is exactly the sort he likes. He wishes he was good enough for her. Many women have thought him good enough for anything; many, he is afraid, good-for-nothing! What does *she* think? He cannot live without her. It would break his heart never to see her again. He is going away. Will she accompany him?"

And Fanny, who through all the struggles and agitation of the fish preserves the *sang-froid* of the fisherman, answers demurely that "*she* knows what gentlemen are, and that no power on earth should induce her to accompany any man one step on his journey through life, whatever his attractions might be or her own feelings (for women were very weak, you know), except as his wife."

"As my wife of course!" gasps the Captain, prepared to pay the highest price for indulgence of his whim, and meaning at the moment, honestly enough, what he proposes.

Miss Draper having now got what she wants—a real offer from a real gentleman—considers she has attained a sufficient social triumph, and prepares to back out of the position with as little offence as possible to the self-love of her admirer.

"It might have been once," she says, shaking her head, and shooting a look at him from under her eyelashes, of which she has often calculated the exact power at the same range—"it can never be now; at least, it would have to be a long while first. I won't talk about my own feelings" (Miss Draper always lets her lovers down very easy), "and I'm sure I'll try to spare yours. Good-bye, Captain! I shall often think of you; and you and I will always be the best of friends, won't we?"

"Always!" exclaims the Captain; and seizing her hand, presses it to his lips.

*　　　*　　　*　　　*

At this stage of her reflections the waning fire, on which she gazes, falls in with a crash; but it fails to disturb the invalid; neither is it that sudden noise which causes Miss Draper to start as if she was stung, and turn to the bed with her eyes full of tears, murmuring—

"I couldn't, I couldn't, my darling! and you lying there! Oh, spare him! spare him! If he would only get well—if he would only get well!"

Then she makes up the fire cautiously, so as not to wake him, wondering with a shiver if he will ever wake again, and goes down on her knees by the armchair, burying her face in her hands.

Not for long, though. Already the grey dawn is stealing through the half-closed shutters; already the day has come which the doctor more than hinted would decide his fate. Hark! what is that? A strain of music, borne on the chill morning breeze even to the watcher's ears. She frowns impatiently, and moving swiftly to the window, closes the shutters with a careful hand.

"Beasts! they might wake him!" she mutters below her breath.

Alas! poor Captain Hughes! Not a twinge of regret does she acknowledge for your departure; not a thought does she waste on yourself and your brother officers. Not a moment does she linger to listen to its band, though the depôt of the 250th Regiment is marching off for good-and-all to the tune of "The Girls we leave behind us!"

CHAPTER XVIII.

"HAPPY," says the proverb, "is the wedding that the sun shines on." This is probably as true as most other proverbs. No doubt the sun shone bright over the park and grounds at Oakover on the morning which was to see John Vandeleur for the second time a bridegroom. Everything, including the old housekeeper fifty years in the family, smiled auspiciously on the event. The lawns had been fresh mown, the gravel rolled smooth, the very flowers in the garden seemed to have summoned the brightest autumn tints they could afford, to do honour to the occasion. The servants of course were in new and gorgeous attire, the men rejoicing in a period of irregular work and unlimited beer, the women jubilant in that savage glee with which our natural enemies celebrate every fresh victory gained over constituted authority. Their very ribbons, dazzling and bran-new, quivered with a triumph almost hysterical in its rapture; and from the housekeeper before mentioned, sixty years of age and weighing sixteen stone, to the under-scullery-maid, not yet confirmed, one might have supposed them about to be married to the men of their choice on the spot, one and all.

Stock jokes, good wishes, hopeful forebodings, were rife in the household; and John Vandeleur, shaving in his dressing-room, looked from his own worn face in the glass, to the keen edge of his razor, with a grim, unearthly smile.

"Would it not be better," he muttered—"better both for her and for me? What right have I to expect that this venture should succeed when all the others failed? And yet—I don't think I ever cared for any of them as I do for this girl—except perhaps Margaret—poor, gentle, loving Margaret! and I had to lay her in her grave! No, I could not stand such another 'facer' as that. If I thought I must go through such a day's work again, I'd get out of it all—now, this moment, with a turn of the wrist and a minute's choke, like a fellow gargling for a sore throat! How surprised they'd all be! That ass of a valet of mine, I'll lay two to one he'd strop my razor before he gave the alarm. And those pretty bridesmaids, with their turquoise lockets! And old Welby—gentlemanlike old fellow, Welby! It wouldn't astonish him so much : he was one of us once. And poor Norah! She'd get over it, though, and marry Gerard Ainslie after all. Not if I know it! No, no, my boy! I'm not going to throw the game into your hands like that! If I was but fifteen years younger, or even ten, I'd hold my own with any of you! Ah, there was a time when John Vandeleur could run most of you at even weights for the Ladies' Plate ; and now, I don't believe she half cares for me! While I—blast me for an old fool!—I love the very gloves she wears! There's one of them in that drawer now! She might do what she liked with me. I could be a better man with her—I know I've got it in me. How happy we might be together! Haven't I everything in the world women like to possess? And what sort of a use have I made of my advantages? I've had a deal of fun, to be sure; but hang me if I'd do the same again! I should like to turn over a new leaf on my wedding-morning. Some fellows would go down on their knees and pray. I wish I could!"

Why didn't he? why couldn't he? It would have been his only chance, and he let it slip. He finished dressing instead, and went down-stairs to inspect the preparations for his bride's welcome when she came home. Except when he swore at the groom of the chambers about some flower-vases, the servants thought he was in high good-humour; and the upper-housemaid—a tall person of experience, who had refused several offers—considered him not a day too old for a bridegroom.

The wedding was to take place at Marston, and the breakfast to be given in the Rectory by the bride's father, who was to officiate at the altar, and offer up his daughter like a second Agamemnon : the simile was his own. Afterwards the happy couple were to proceed at once to Oakover, there to spend their honeymoon and remain during the winter. This last was an arrangement of Vandeleur's, who, having been married before, was alive to the discomfort of a continental trip for two people whose acquaintance is, after all, none of the most intimate, and to whom the privacy and comfort of a home seem almost indispensable. He had earned his experience,

and determined to profit by it. This, you will observe,
young ladies, is one of the advantages of marrying a
widower.

It is needless to relate that at the wedding-breakfast were congregated the smartest and best-dressed
people of the neighbourhood. Even those who had
hitherto disapproved of his goings-on, and kept aloof
from his society, were too glad to welcome a man
of Mr. Vandeleur's acres and position back into the
fold of respectability. There is joy even on earth
over a repentant sinner, provided that he leaves off
bachelor-ways, opens his house, gives solemn dinners,
and breaks out with an occasional ball !

Lady Baker was triumphant. " She had always
said there was a deal of good in Vandeleur, that
only wanted bringing out. Wild oats, my dear !
Well, young men will sow them plentifully, you
know; and neither Newmarket nor Paris are what
you can call good schools. Poor Sir Philip always
said so, and he was a thorough man of the world—a
thorough man of the world, my dear ; and liked Mr.
Vandeleur, what he knew of him, very much. To be
sure they never met but twice. Ah ! there was
twenty years' difference between him and me, and I
daresay there's more between this couple. Well, I

always think a wife should be younger than her husband. And she's sweetly pretty, isn't she, Jane? Though I can't say I like the shape of her wreath, and I never saw anybody look so deadly pale in my life."

Thus Lady Baker to her next neighbour at the wedding-breakfast, Miss Tregunter, looking very fresh and wholesome in white and blue, with the sweetest turquoise-locket (Mr. Vandeleur had eight of them made for the eight bridesmaids) that ever rose and fell on the soft bosom of one of these pretty officials unattached. Miss Tregunter, knowing she is in her best looks, has but one regret, that she is not dressed in pink, for she sits next to Dolly Egremont.

This young gentleman is in the highest possible state of health and spirits. He has been up for his examination, and failed to pass; which, however, does not in the least affect his peace of mind, as he entertains no intention of trying again. He and Burton, who has been more fortunate, and is about to be gazetted to a commission in the Household Troops at once, have come to pay their old tutor a visit expressly for the wedding. They consider themselves gentlemen-at-large now, and finished men of the world.

Carrying out this idea, they assume an air of proprie-
torship in their relations with the young ladies of the
party, which, though inexpressibly offensive to its
male portion, is tolerated with considerable forbearance, and even approval, by the fairer guests, especially the bridesmaids. That distinguished body
has behaved with the greatest steadiness at church,
earning unqualified approval from the most competent
judges, such as clerk and sexton, by its fixed attention to the Marriage Service, no less than from the
fascinating uniformity of its appearance and the
perfection of its drill. It is now, to a certain extent,
broken up and scattered about; for its duties as
a disciplined force are nearly over, and each of
its rank-and-file relapses naturally into her normal
state of private warfare and individual aggression
on the common enemy.

Miss Tregunter, placed between Dolly Egremont
and Dandy Burton, with white soup in her plate
and champagne in her glass, is a fair specimen of
the rest.

"Isn't she lovely?" whispers this young lady,
as in duty bound, glancing at the bride, and arrang-
ing her napkin carefully over her blue and white
draperies.

Dolly steals a look at Norah, sitting pale and stately at the cross-table between her father and her husband. He cannot help thinking of Gerard's favourite song, and that reminds him of Gerard. A twinge takes his honest heart, while he reflects that he would not like to see Miss Tregunter in a wreath of orange-blossoms sitting by anybody but himself; and that perhaps poor Ainslie would be very unhappy if he were here. But this is no time for sadness. Glasses are jingling, plates clattering, servants hurrying about, and tongues wagging with that enforced merriment which is so obvious at all entertainments of a like nature. We gild our wed-ding-feasts with splendour, we smother them in flowers, and swamp them in wine; yet, somehow, though the Death's-head is necessarily a guest at all our banquets, we are never so conscious of his pre-sence as on these special occasions of festivity and rejoicing.

"Wants a little more colour to be perfection," answers cunning Dolly, with a glance into his com-panion's rosy face. "I don't admire your sickly beau-ties—'Quenched in the chaste beams of the watery moon; Whitewash I never condescend to spoon.' Ain't I romantic, Miss Tregunter, and poetical?"

"Ain't you a goose!" answers the bridesmaid, laughing. "And I don't believe you know what you do admire!"

"I admire blue and white, with a turquoise locket," interposes Dandy Burton from the other side. He too entertains a vague and undefined penchant for Miss Tregunter, who is an heiress.

"Well, you're in luck!" answers the young lady, "for you've eight of us to stare at. Hush! Mr. Welby's going to speak. I hope he won't break down."

Then there is a great deal of knocking of knife-handles on the table, and murmurs of "Hear, hear;" while all the faces turn with one movement, as if pulled by a string, towards Mr. Welby, who is standing up, almost as pale as his daughter, and whose thin hands tremble so that he can scarcely steady them against the fork with which he is scoring marks on the white cloth.

He calls on his guests to fill their glasses. The gentlemen help the ladies, with a good deal of simpering on both sides. A coachman acting footman breaks a trifle-dish, and stands aghast at his own awkwardness. But, notwithstanding this diversion, everybody's attention is again fastened on poor Mr. Welby, who shakes more and more.

"I have a toast to propose," he says; and everybody repeats, "Hear! hear!" "A toast you will all drink heartily, I am sure. There are some subjects on which the dullest man cannot help being eloquent. Some on which the most eloquent must break down. I ought not to be afraid of my own voice. I have heard it once a week for a good many years; but now I cannot say half I mean, and I feel you will expect no long sermon from me to-day. I have just confided to my oldest friend the earthly happiness of my only child. You all know him, and I need not enlarge upon his popularity, his talents, his social successes, and his worth. Why should I tell you my opinion of him? Have I not an hour ago, in the discharge of my sacred office as a priest, and with such blessings as only a father's heart can call down, given him the very apple of mine eye, the very light of my lonely home? May she be as precious to him as she has been to me!" Here Mr. Welby's own voice became very hoarse; and noses were blown at intervals, down each side of the table. "Of her? What shall I say of her?" His accents were low and broken now, while he only got each sentence out with difficulty, bit by bit. "Why,—that if she

proves but half as good a wife to him—as she has
been—a daughter to me—he may thank God every
night and morning from a full heart, for the happiness of his lot. I call upon you to drink the healths
of Mr. and Mrs. Vandeleur!"

How all the guests nodded and drank and cheered
till the very blossoms shook on the wedding-cake,
and their voices failed! Only Dolly forgot to nod
or drink or cheer, so eagerly was his attention fixed
upon the bride.

Brave Norah never looked at her father, never
looked at her husband, never looked up from her
plate, nor moved a muscle of her countenance, but
sat still and solemn and grave, like a beautiful statue.
Only when the speaker's feelings got the better
of him large tears welled up slowly, slowly, into
her eyes, and dropped one by one on the bouquet
that lay in her lap. Dolly could have cried too,
for that silent, sad, unearthly quietude seemed to
him more piteous, more touching, than any amount
of flurry and tears and hysterical laughter and
natural agitation.

In talking it over afterwards, people only protested "how beautifully Mr. Vandeleur had behaved!" And no doubt that accomplished gentleman

said and did exactly the right thing at the moment
and under the circumstances. A felon in the dock
is hardly in a more false position than a bridegroom at his own wedding breakfast. He feels,
indeed, very much as if he had stolen something, and
everybody knew he was the thief. I appeal to all
those who have experienced the trial, whether it does
not demand an extreme of tact and courage to avoid
masking the prostration and despondency under
which a man cannot but labour in such a predica-
ment, by an ill-timed flippancy which everybody in
the room feels to be impertinence of the worst
possible taste.

Mr. Vandeleur, though he never liked to look a
single individual in the face, had no shyness on an
occasion like the present. He was well dressed, well
got-up, in good spirits, and felt that he had gained
at least ten years on old Time to-day. He glanced
proudly down on his bride, kindly and respectfully
at her father, pleasantly round on the assembled
guests; touched frankly and cordially on the good
will these displayed; alluded feelingly to Mr.
Welby's affection for his daughter; neither said
too much nor too little about his own sentiments;
humbly hoped he might prove worthy of the bless-

ing he should strive hard to deserve; and ended by calling on Dandy Burton, as the youngest man present—or, at all events, the one with the smartest neckcloth—to propose the health of the brides-maids.

It was a good speech,—everybody said so ; good feeling, good taste, neither too grave nor too gay. Everybody except Burton, who found himself in an unexpected fix, from which there could be no escape. The Dandy was not shy, but for the space of at least five minutes he wished himself a hundred miles off. Neither did Miss Tregunter help him in the least. On the contrary, she looked up at him when he rose, with a comic amazement, and unfeeling derision in her rosy face, which it was well calculated to ex-press, but which confused him worse and worse.

So he fingered his glass, and shifted from one leg to the other, and hemmed and hawed, and at last got out his desire " to propose the health of the bridesmaids—whose dresses had been the admira-tion of the beholders ; who, one and all, were only second in beauty to the bride ; and who had per-formed their part so well. He was quite sure he expressed the feelings of every one present in hoping to see them act equally creditably at no distant date on a similar occasion;" and so sat down in a state of intense confusion, under the scowls of the young ladies, the good-natured silence of the gentlemen, and an audible whisper from Miss Tregunter, that "she never heard anybody make such a mess of anything in her life!"

Somebody must return thanks for the bridesmaids; and a whisper creeping round the tables soon rose to a shout of "Mr. Egremont! Mr. Egremont! Go it, Dolly! Speak up! It's all in your line! No quotations!" It brought Dolly to his legs; and he endeavoured to respond with the amount of merriment and facetiousness required. But no; it would not come. That pale face with the slowly-dropping tears still haunted him; and whilst he could fix his thoughts on nothing else, he dared not look again in the direction of the bride. He blundered, indeed, through a few of the usual empty phrases and vapid compliments. He identified himself with the bundle of beauty for which he spoke; he only regretted not being a bridesmaid, because if he were, he could never possibly be a bridegroom. He lamented, like a hypocrite, as Miss Tregunter well knew, the difficulty of choosing from so dazzling an assemblage, and concluded by thanking Burton, in the name of the young ladies he represented, for his good wishes on future occasions of a similar nature, but suggested that perhaps if they came to the altar "one at a time, it would last the longer, and might prove a more interesting ceremony to each."

Still Dolly's heart was heavy; and misgivings of evil, such as he had never entertained before, clouded his genial humour, and almost brought the tears to his eyes. Even when the "happy couple" drove off, and he threw an old shoe for luck after their carriage, something seemed to check his outstretched arm, something seemed to whisper in his ear, that for all the bright sunshine and the smiling sky a dark cloud lowered over the pale proud head of the beautiful bride; and that for Norah Vandeleur ancient customs, kindly superstitions, and good wishes, were all in vain.

CHAPTER XIX.

FOR WORSE.

Mr. Bruff was a kind-hearted fellow. To their credit be it spoken, actors and actresses, although so familiar with fictitious sorrow and excitement, are of all people the most sensitive to cases of real distress. Many a morning had Mr. Bruff waited anxiously for Mrs. Briggs, to hear her report of the young officer's health; and at last, when that worthy woman informed him, with a radiant face, that the patient was what she called "on the turn," he shook both her hands with such vehemence that she felt persuaded she had made a conquest, and began to reflect on the prudence of marrying again, being well-to-do in the world, and not much past fifty years of age. She had, however, many other matters on her mind just at present. From the time Gerard recovered consciousness, Fanny was never in his room except while he slept, though she continually pervaded the passage, poor girl, with a pale face, and eager, anxious eyes. On Mrs. Briggs, therefore, devolved the nursing of the invalid; a duty she undertook with extreme good-will and that energy which seldom deserts a woman who is continually cleaning her own house, and "tidying up," both above-stairs and below.

She wished, though, she had put on a smarter cap, when Mr. Bruff tapped at the door, to present his compliments, with kind inquiries, good wishes, and yesterday's paper—not very clean, and tainted by tobacco-smoke, but calculated, nevertheless, to en-liven the leisure of an invalid in an armchair.

Gerard was this morning out of bed for the first time. Mrs. Briggs had got him up; had washed, dressed, and would even have shaved him, but that the young chin could well dispense with such atten-tion. No contrast could be much greater than that of the wan, delicate, emaciated invalid by the fire, and the square, black-browed, rough-looking, red-nosed sympathiser in the passage.

Mrs. Briggs, with her sleeves tucked up, and apron girded round her waist, kept the door ajar,

and so held converse with the visitor, while she
would not permit him to come in. "To-morrow,
Mr. Bruff," said she, graciously, "or the day after,
according as the doctor thinks well. You've a good
heart of your own, though you don't look it! And
he thanks you kindly, does my poor young gentleman, for he's dozing beautiful now, and so do I ; "
slamming the door thereafter in his face, and returning with the newspaper to her charge. "And you
may thank heaven on your knees, my dear," continued the landlady, who liked to improve an occasion, and was never averse to hear herself talk, " as
you're sitting alive and upright in that there cheer
this blessed day. You may thank heaven, and the
young woman upstairs, as was with you when they
brought you in, and never left you, my dear, day
and night, till you took your turn, no more nor if
she'd been your sister or your sweetheart ! "

"What ! I've been very bad, have I ? " asked
Gerard, still a good deal confused, and conscious
chiefly of great weakness and a languor not wholly
unpleasant.

"Bad ! " echoed Mrs. Briggs. " It's death's-door
as you've been nigh, my dear, to the very scraper.
And when we'd all lost heart, and even Doctor

Driver looked as black as night, and shook his head
solemn, it was only the young woman upstairs as
kep' us up, for we can't spare him, says she, an' we
won't, as pale as death, an' as fixed as fate. An'
Doctor Driver says, says he, ' If ever a young gentleman was kep' alive by careful nursing, why, my
dear, it was your own self, through this last ten days,
an' that's the girl as done it ! ' "

"Where is she ? " exclaimed Gerard, eagerly,
and with a changing colour, that showed how weak
he was. "I've never thanked her. Can't I see
her at once ? What a brute she must think me ! "

"Patience, my dear," said motherly Mrs. Briggs.
"It isn't likely as the young woman would come
in now you're so much better, till you was up and
dressed. But if you'll promise to take your
chicken-broth like a good young gentleman, why
I daresay as the young woman will bring it up
for you. And I must go and see about it now, this
minute, for I dursn't trust H'Ann. So you take
a look of your paper there, and keep your mind
easy, my dear, `for you're getting better nicely
now, though it's good food and good nursing as
you require, and good food and good nursing I'll
take care as you get."

So Mrs. Briggs scuttled off to her own especial department below-stairs, pleased with the notion that a touching little romance was going on in her humble dwelling, fostered by the combined influences of convalescence, contiguity, and chicken-broth. She felt favourably disposed towards her invalid, towards his nurse, towards Mr. Bruff, towards the world in general,—even towards the negligent and constantly erring H'Ann.

Gerard, left alone, tried, of course, to walk across the room, and was surprised to find that he could not so much as stand without holding by the table. Even after so trifling an exertion he was glad to return to his chair, and sank back to read his newspaper, with a sigh of extreme contentment and repose.

Its columns seemed to recall at once that world which had so nearly slipped away. He skipped the leading article, indeed, but would probably have missed it had he been in high health, and proceeded to those lighter subjects which it required little mental effort to master or comprehend. He read a couple of police reports and a divorce case; learned that a scientific gentleman had propounded a new theory about aërolites; and tried

to realise a distressing accident (nine lives lost)
on the Mersey. Then he rested a little, plunged
into a more comfortable attitude, and turned the
sheet for a look at the other side.

There was half a column of births, deaths, and
marriages, and he was languidly pitying Felix
Bunney, Esq , of The Warren, whose lady had produced twins, when, casting his eye a little lower
down, he read the following announcement:—" On
the — instant, at Marston Rectory, ——-shire, by the
Reverend William Welby, father of the bride,
Leonora, only daughter of the above, to John Vandeleur, Esq., of Oakover, in the same county, and
—— Square, London, S.W." His head swam.
That was bodily weakness, of course ! But though
the printed letters danced up and down the paper,
he made an effort, and read it over carefully, word
by word, once more. His first feeling, strange to
say, was of astonishment that he could bear the
blow so well ; that he was not stunned, prostrated,
driven mad outright ! Perhaps his very weakness
was in his favour ; perhaps the extreme bodily lassi-
tude to which he was reduced deprived him of the
power to suffer intensely, and the poor bruised reed
bent under a blast that would have crushed some

thriving standard plant cruelly to the earth.. He
realised the whole scene of the wedding, though its
figures wavered before his eyes like a dream. He
could see the grave father and priest in his long,
sweeping vesture; the manly, confident face of Mr.
Vandeleur, with its smile of triumph; the bonny
bridesmaids circling round the altar; and Norah,
pale, stately, beautiful, with that fatal wreath on her
fair young brow, and her transparent veil floating
like a mist about the glorious form that he had hoped
against hope some day to make his own. Fool!
fool! could he blame her? What right had he to
suppose she was to waste her youth and beauty on
a chance, and wait years for him? He ought to
have known it. He ought to have expected it.
But it was hard to bear. Hard, hard, to bear!
Particularly now! Then he leaned his head on the
table, and wept freely—bitterly. Poor fellow! he
was weakened, you see, by illness, and not himself,
or he would surely never have given way like this.
After a while he rallied, for the lad did not want
courage, and, weak as he was, summoned up pride
to help him. I think it hurt him then more than
at first. Presently he grew angry, as men often do
when very sorrowful, and turned fiercely against the

love he had so cherished for months, vowing that it was all feverish folly and illusion, a boy's malady, that must be got over and done with before he enters upon a man's work. He ought to have known the truth long ago. He had read of such things in his Ovid, in his Lemprière, in Thackeray's biting pages, clandestinely devoured at study-hours, beneath a volume of Whewell's Dynamics, or Gibbon's Roman Empire. *Varium et mutabile* seemed the verdict alike of Latin love-poet and classical referee; while the English novelist, whose sentiments so strangely influence both young and old, spoke of the subject with a grim pity, half in sorrow, half in anger, excusing with quaint phrases, and pathetic humour, the inconstancy of her whose very nature it is to be fascinated by novelty and subject to the influence of change.

"I suppose women are all so!" concluded the invalid, with a sigh; and then he remembered Mother Briggs's account of his accident, and his illness; of the nurse that had tended him so indefatigably and so devotedly; wondering who she was, and what she was, when he was likely to see her, whether she was pretty, and why she was there.

Notwithstanding all this, he began to read over the paragraph about the wedding once again, when there came a tap, and the bump of a tray against his door. The chicken-broth now made its appearance, flanked by long strips of toast, and borne by a comely young woman quietly dressed, whom he recognised at once as his former fishing acquaintance, Miss Draper of Ripley Mill.

Fanny's beauty, always of the florid order, had not suffered from watching and anxiety. On the contrary, it appeared more refined and delicate than of old ; nor, though she had been very pale in the passage, was there any want of colour in her face while she set down the tray. Never in her life had she blushed so scarlet, never trembled and turned away before from the face of man.

He half rose, in natural courtesy, but his knees would not keep straight, and he was fain to sit down again. She came round behind him, and busied herself in settling the pillows of his chair.

"Miss Draper," he began, trying to turn and look her in the face, "what must you think of me? Never to have recognised you! Never to have thanked you! I only heard to-day of all your kindness ; and till you came in this moment, I had

not found out who it was that nursed me. I must
have been very ill indeed not to know *you*."

Weak and faint as it came, it was the same voice
that so won on her, that soft summer's day, when
the Mayfly was on Ripley-water. It was the same
kindly, gentle, high-bred manner that acted on the
low-born woman like a charm.

" You have been very ill, sir," she murmured, still
keeping behind him. "You frightened us all for a
day or two. It's heaven's mercy you came through."

He sighed. Was he thinking that for him it
would have been more merciful never to have
recovered a consciousness that only made him
vulnerable? Better to have been carried down the
lodging-house stairs in his coffin, than to walk out
on his feet, with the knowledge that Norah Vandeleur was lost to him for ever! But he could not
be ungrateful, and his voice trembled with real feeling, while he said, " It is not only heaven's mercy,
but your care, that has saved me. You must not
think I don't feel it. It seems so absurd for a fellow
not to be able to stand up. I—I can't say half as
much as I should like."

Still behind him, still careful that he should not
see her face, though there were no blushes to hide

now. Indeed she had grown very pale again. Her
voice, too, was none of the steadiest, while she
assumed the nurse's authority once more, and bade
him begin on his chicken-broth without delay.

" I know it's good," said she, " for I helped to
make it. Both Mrs. Briggs and Doctor Driver say
you must have plenty of nourishment. Hadn't you
better eat it before it's cold ? "

Convalescence in early manhood means the hunger
of the wolf. He obeyed at once ; and Fanny, fairly
turning her back on him, looked steadfastly out of the
window.

I do not know why there should be less romance
in the consumption of chicken-broth by an Infantry
ensign than in the cutting of bread and butter by
a German maiden, with blue eyes, flaxen hair, and
well-developed form. It all depends upon the
accessories. I am not sure but that on reflection
most of us would be forced to admit that the ten-
derest moments of our lives are connected in some
manner with the act of eating and drinking. Of
all ways to the heart, the shortest seems, perhaps,
to be down the throat. In the higher classes, what
a deal of love-making is carried on at dinner parties,
pic-nics, above all, ball-suppers. In the middle,

a suitor never feels that he is progressing satis-
factorily till he is asked to tea; and in the lower,
although bread and cheese as well as bacon may
prove non-conductors, a good deal of business, no
doubt, is done through the agency of beer! " Venus
perishes," says the Latin proverb, " without the
assistance of Bacchus and Ceres." Nor, although
I am far from disputing that love-fits may be con-
tracted so violent as to prove incurable even by
starvation, have I any doubt that the disease is more
fatal to a full man than one fasting. In other words,
that few admirers, if any, are so attentive, so plas-
tic, so playful, altogether so agreeable, before breakfast as after dinner.

Gerard finished every crumb of his toast and every
drop of his chicken-broth undisturbed. The avidity
with which he ate was in itself the best possible
omen of returning health and strength; and yet
Fanny still looked out at window, on the dull deserted street. Even the tinkling of his spoon in
the empty basin did not serve to arrest her attention, and he would have gone and shaken her by the
hand, to thank her once more for her kindness, but
that he knew he could not walk those three paces to
save his life.

His pocket-handkerchief was on the chimney-piece; he wanted it, and could not reach it. Nothing was more natural than that he should ask his nurse to hand it him, neither was it possible for her to refuse compliance; but as their fingers met, although she tried hard to keep her face averted, he could not but see that the tears were streaming down her cheeks—tears, as his own heart told him, of joy and thanksgiving for his safety—tears of pity and affection—and of love.

He clasped the hand that touched his own, and drew her towards him. "Miss Draper—Fanny!" said he, never a word more, and she flung herself down on her knees, and buried her face on his arm, bursting out sobbing as if her heart would break; and then he knew it all—all;—the whole sad story from the beginning of their acquaintance—the ill-matched, ill-conceived attachment out of which happiness could never come! He pitied her, he soothed her, he stroked her glossy hair, he bent his own face down to hers.

"I love you! I love you!" she sobbed out wildly. "I loved you from the first—the day we walked together by Ripley-water. I can't help it. It's too late now. If you had died, I should have died too. If you go away and leave me, I'll break my heart. Oh! if I was a lady! If only I was a lady! Why shouldn't I be?"

He was weakened by illness. He was alone in the world now. His heart, all sore and quivering, was painfully sensitive to the touch of consolation and affection. What wonder if he suffered his wiser nature to be overborne ; what wonder if he accepted all that was so lavishly poured out at his feet, and shutting his eyes wilfully to consequences, promised Fanny Draper that she should be "a lady" as soon as ever he was strong enough to stand up and say "amen" in a church?

Mr. Bruff, could he have obtained admittance, might have taken a very pretty lesson in stage love-making during the next half-hour. Gerard Ainslie, lending himself willingly to that which he knew all the time was an illusion, vowed to his own heart that he was acting nobly, honourably, chivalrously, according to the dictates of gratitude, and as in duty bound ; while Fanny Draper, in love for the first time in her life, felt she had gained everything hitherto desired by her ill-regulated fancy, and was ready, nay, willing, to take the consequences of her venture, be they what they might.

CHAPTER XX.

THE HONEYMOON.

There was a pretty little room at Oakover, opening by a French window into a sheltered flower-garden, which Mrs. Vandeleur had voted from the very first especially adapted for a breakfast-parlour. Its bright paper, pretty furniture, choice engravings, and, above all, abundance of light, afforded every encouragement to that cheerfulness of mood and feelings with which it is advisable to begin the day. It must have been an obstinate fit of ill-humour to resist all these accessories, assisted by a glimpse of sunshine, a well-served breakfast, and a comfortable fire.

Into this pleasant apartment stepped Mr. Vandeleur about ten o'clock in the morning towards the conclusion of that sequestered period termed

conventionally his honeymoon, but on the bridegroom's worn face sat an expression of restlessness
and discontent in keeping neither with time nor
place. He walked up to the fire, seized the poker,
gave a savage dig at the coals, and rang the bell
with a short, stern jerk that brought the smoothest
and politest of servants to the door in less than
thirty seconds. They were all a good deal afraid
of him below-stairs, and it is needless to say
nobody was better waited on than the master of
Oakover.

"Has Mrs. Vandeleur been down?" said he,
glancing impatiently at the unused breakfast-service.

"I think not, sir," answered the domestic respectfully, "but Miss Glancer's just come from her
room, and I'll inquire."

"Tell her to go up again and let her mistress
know breakfast is ready," said his master sternly,
and walked off to the window muttering, not so low
but that the servant overheard—

"Not down yet! She never is down when I am!
To be sure, Glancer's the worst maid in Europe. I
can see that with half an eye. And a saucy, trouble-
some jade into the bargain. Margaret always used
to breakfast with me. But this one—this one!

I wonder whether I've been a cursed fool? Sometimes I think I have!"

Then Mr. Vandeleur, taking no notice of his
breakfast, nor the unopened letters piled beside
his plate, whistled, shook his head, thrust his hands
into his pockets, and looked out at window.

It was late autumn, almost early winter, and a
coating of hoar-frost still lay crisp and white where
the lawn was sheltered by an angle of the building
from the sun. Such flowers as had not been removed
were sadly blackened by the cold; while, though
the tan and russet hues of the waning year still
clothed their lower branches, the topmost twigs of
the trees cut bare and leafless against the deep,
blue, dazzling sky. The scene without was bright,
clear, and beautiful; but chilling, hard, and cheerless, all the same.

Perhaps it was the more in keeping with certain
reflections of the proprietor within. For five
minutes he stood motionless, looking steadfastly
at a presumptuous robin smirking and sidling and
pruning itself on the gravel-walk.

In that five minutes how many by-gone scenes did
he conjure up! How many years, how much of an
ill-spent lifetime, did he travel back into the past!

London, in the heyday of youth, and health, and
hope. Fashion, position, popularity, smiles of
beauty, smiles of fortune, social and material success
of every kind. Paris, in the prime of manhood,
when the gilt was perhaps a little off the ginger-
bread, but the food tasted luscious and satisfying
still. More smiles, more beauty ; the smiles franker,
broader, sprightlier ; the beauty less retiring, less
difficult to please. Then England once more, with
its field-sports, its climate, its comforts, its con-
veniences ; the boon companions, the jovial gatherings, the liberty, even the license of a bachelor in
a country home. After that, marriage. Spirits
still buoyant, health still unbroken, and the dear
fragile, devoted, tender wife, of whom, even now,
here waiting for his bride to breakfast with him, he
could not think without a gnawing pain about his
heart !

His bride ! The one woman of his whole life
whom he had most desired to win. Not to please
his fancy, as he knew too well ; not to minister to
his vanity ; but—and he smiled to think he was
using the language of idiotic romance and drawing-
room poetry, of unfledged boys and boarding-school
girls—to satisfy his longing to be loved. He, the

used-up, worn-out, grizzled old reprobate! What business had he, as he asked himself, grinning and clenching his hands, what business had he with hopes and fancies like these? After such a life as his, was he to be rewarded at last by the true affection of a pure and spotless woman? If there was such a thing as retribution in this world, what had he a right to expect? Dared he tell her a tenth, a hundredth of his follies, his iniquities, his crimes? Could he look into those guileless eyes, and not blush with very shame at his own memories? Could he rest his head on that white sinless breast, and not quiver with remorse, self-scorn, and self-reproach? Still, if she did but love him, if she could but love him, he felt there was a chance for repentance and amendment; he felt there was hope even for him.

If she could but love him. Alas! he was beginning to fear she had not learned to love him yet.

A quiet step in the passage, the rustle of a dress, and Norah entered the room. Norah, looking twice as beautiful as on the wedding morning, though still far too pale and grave and stately for a bride. Her deep eyes had always something of melancholy in them, but they were deeper and darker than

ever of late; while on the chiseled features of the
fair, proud face, for months had been settling an
expression of repressed feeling and enforced composure, that caused it to look tranquil, reserved, and
matronly beyond its years.

She was beautifully dressed, though in somewhat
sober colours for a bride, and as Vandeleur turned
round on her entrance, his eyes could not but be
pleased with the folds of falling drapery that marked
while they enhanced the faultless outline of her
shape.

She passed his letters with scarcely a glance,
though the uppermost of the pile was addressed in
a hand, feeble, delicate, scrawling, not to be mis-
taken for a man's. Few wives so lately married
but would have betrayed some curiosity as to the
correspondent. Norah saw nothing, it would seem,
and suspected nothing, for she sat down before the
urn without a word, and proceeded to make tea in
a somewhat listless manner, now becoming habitual.

"You're late, my dear," said Vandeleur, seating
himself, too, and proceeding to open his letters.

"Am I?" she replied, absently. "I'm afraid
I'm very lazy. And I don't sleep so well as I
used."

It was true enough. I suppose nobody does sleep well who is haunted by a sense of having acted unfairly towards two other people, and having lost at the same time all the hopes once glowing so brightly in the future. Norah's slumbers were broken, no doubt, and though

"The name she dared not name by day"

was never on her lips in her waking hours, the phantom of its owner, with sad, reproachful eyes, paid her perhaps many an unwelcome visit in the visions of the night.

She went on quietly with her breakfast, taking no more notice of her husband, till a burst of repressed laughter caused her to look up astonished, and she observed him convulsed with a merriment peculiar to himself, that from some unexplained cause always impressed her with a sense of fear.

Vandeleur had started slightly when he opened the topmost letter of his pile. He had not at first recognised the handwriting, so much had some dozen lessons and a few weeks' painstaking done for his correspondent, but the signature set all doubt at rest, while the matter of the epistle seemed to afford

food for considerable mirth and approbation, denoted
by such half-spoken expressions as the following :—

"Clever girl!" "How right I was!" "I said
she would if she had the chance!" "What an
inconceivable young fool!" "I know it! I know
it!" "You deserve as much again, and you shall
have it by return of post!"

The letter was indeed explicit enough. It ran as
follows :—

"HONOURED SIR,—In accordance with my promise, I now take up my pen to apprise you that
everything has been arranged as I have reason to
believe you desired, and you will see by the signature below that my earthly happiness is now
assured and complete. Sir, it was but last week as
I became the lawful wife of Mr. Ainslie, and I lose
no time in acquainting you with the same. I am
indeed a happy woman, though you will not care
to hear this—perhaps will not believe that I speak
the truth. As heaven is above me, I declare my
Gerard is all and everything I can wish. Sir, I
would not change places with any woman in the
world.

"He has met with a serious accident in a fall

from his horse, and been very bad, as you may have
heard, but is doing well now, and with my nursing
will soon be strong and hearty again. We are
living in lodgings at the same address. Of course
I have been put to considerable expense, particularly
at first, but I am aware that I can safely trust your
generous promise, and fulfilment of what you said
you would do.

"Mr. Vandeleur,—Sir,—Do not laugh at me ; I
love my husband very dearly, and nothing shall
ever come between us now.

"Your dutiful and obliged

"FANNY AINSLIE."

"Capital! capital ! " exclaimed Vandeleur when
he reached the end. "'Pon my soul, it's too absurd,
too ludicrous ! What will the world come to next?"

"Something seems to amuse you," observed
Norah, quietly. "If it's no secret, suppose you
tell it me—I feel this morning as if a laugh would
do me good."

"Secret ! my dear," repeated Vandeleur. "It
won't be a secret long. Certainly not if newspapers
and parish registers tell the truth. It would seem
incredible, only I have it from the lady herself.

Such a lady! I should think she couldn't spell her own name six weeks ago. Would you believe it, Norah? That young fool, Gerard Ainslie, has been and married a girl you remember down here, called Fanny Draper. A bold tawdry girl who used to be always hanging about Ripley Mill. Here's her letter! You can read it if you like!"

He looked very hard at Norah while he gave it, but his wife never moved an eyelash, taking it from his hand coldly and impenetrably as if it had been an egg or a teaspoon. With the same fixed face and impassive manner she read it through from end to end, and returned it, observing only in a perfectly unmoved voice—

"I believe she loves him. It is an unfortunate marriage, but I hope he will be happy."

Mrs. Vandeleur appeared, however, less amused than her husband, nor do I think she took this opportunity of enjoying the laugh she thought would do her so much good on that cold frosty morning at Oakover.

END OF VOL. I.

PRINTED BY VIRTUE AND CO., CITY ROAD, LONDON.

www.ingramcontent.com/pod-product-compliance
Lightning Source LLC
Chambersburg PA
CBHW020349030726
47496CB00007B/2072